My Stories
Have
No Endings

My Stories
Have
No Endings

a novel

Gayle Gonsalves

Enjoy These words +
the journey they bring
Gayle   Apr 2/21

Cover design and typesetting by Lucy Holtsnider.

ISBN 978-1-7774374-1-1

For Nicola

Claim a bonus short story for free!

1. Go to
   gaylegonsalveswriter.com/contact-gayle
2. Share your email address
3. Receive *Tamarind Stew,* a bonus
   short story, straight to your inbox!

Contents

My Stories Have No Endings

I believe the tamarind tree is as beautiful and proud as the breadfruit and flamboyant trees. These three trees have massive trunks and dark bark. They grow high and their limbs stretch into the heavens, yet they are different. The breadfruit tree's distinctive giant leaves yield a perfectly round, large green fruit, unique in texture and flavour. The canopy of the flamboyant tree produces a stunning red flower that leaves me gasping for breath, with its bold colour and sweet fragrance. When this tree is in bloom, the island of Antigua is transformed by its

imposing beauty as it casts a magical spell on the land—
its bright red flowers light up the landscape.

The tamarind tree is different. Its large branches have
small leaves, and it bears a nondescript, brown pod that
holds its fruit. This tree does not have a beautiful blossom;
it doesn't deceive you that it will yield anything but a
bittersweet fruit. Yet it is from this tree that Antiguans
make a delicacy called tamarind stew.

In Antigua, we experience one season. The days are an
unending cycle of sun dotted with the occasional burst of
rain. This sun makes trees grow, flowers blossom and fruit
ripen. It gives the island its unending lushness, so that it
looks like a ripe fruit ready to burst. On this little island,
we mark time by the temperature of the sea and the
seasons of our fruits. In the humid months of June and
July, when the sea is hot, mangoes are in full bloom, and
at Christmas we don't go to the beach—the water is too
cold—but the land bears sugar apples. Tamarinds come
into season around May, when the water begins to warm
and we again enjoy the sea.

Today the tamarind tree is in bloom, and I step into
the yard and pick one of its pods. I hold the long, brown
tubular fruit in my hand. It's been seven years since
Hayden and I threw rocks into the branches and gleefully
watched the tamarinds fall. Back then, we'd scramble to
put them in a bag. If we felt lazy, we'd lie under the tree,
enjoying the cool shade, imagining images in the puffy
white clouds. And if we were in a hurry, the two of us

dashed inside my home to shell the tamarinds and make our favourite delicacy. I know the Ancestors are alive and they talk. Their spirits reside in the trees. Not everyone hears the voices of the past. I am one who does. It is a gift. Their sounds are there, but few know how to bend themselves into the wind to listen for their whisper. As keen as my ear is, those whispers never explained why a day would come when tamarinds would fall from the tree, and I'd pick them off the ground by myself.

CHAPTER ONE

Scaling Walls

My mother buys me books with pictures of powerful lions, pretty birds and large castles where men and women wear lavish clothes. I climb into her lap and snuggle into her warm body as I intently study the pictures of the enchanted animals and fairy tale characters. As we turn the pages, my eyes delight at the pretty sketches. My small hand touches them, hoping they will jump off the page and become real so I can play with them. Next to the pictures, running close together at the bottom of the page, are small markings. As I inspect them, I notice that they are different, yet similar; the lines

are either straight or slightly curved, and all are around
the same size. I run my small hand over the marks.
I point to them. "What's this?"

My mother shifts in her seat, and being on her lap,
I move as she moves. She doesn't say anything for a
moment.

"What's this?" I ask again.

"Words."

"What's that?"

"Words tell you what's in the picture."

My eyes grow wide with interest. "What you mean?"

"This is a storybook and the words tell the story."

"What is a story?"

"It's like one long nursery rhyme."

"Tell me what it says on this page."

"I can't."

"Why?"

"I don't know how to read."

Then my mother calmly explains that one day I'll go to
school, where I'll learn to read because it's important that
I know the alphabet so that I can have a wonderful life.
I don't hear her speaking because I'm looking intently at
the page. Instinctively, I understand that each letter adds
together to make a word, and words create stories. Since
I can't read, I surprise my mother by making up a story
about the people and animals on the page. My mother
listens and smiles. When I finish with one story, I turn
the page and, seeing new pictures, tell her another tale.

Each night, I sit in my mother's lap and tell my stories. One day the lion is searching for a friend. On another day, he is the strongest animal in the jungle, who wants to eat everyone and everything. I don't know anything about heroes or kings, but I instinctively understand that stories need interesting people. Whenever I create a story, I hear a magical, musical voice in my head, speaking the words, and as I speak, I believe that voice comes to life. My stories never have endings, because I don't know how to finish them; I always invent new ways for the people in my stories to live.

Each day, I look forward to hearing my voice transport me from my home to a vibrant, fascinating land, where I see happy people and colourful costumes. I am in love with this magical voice and truly know that I always want to hear it.

Because I am desperate to learn how to read, I can't wait to start school. Each morning, I look enviously at the kids who pass our house in their well-pressed school uniforms; I cry because I want to join them. I'm so excited when my mother tells me that I'm big enough for school. Finally, I'll learn how to read, and I restlessly count my sleeps until it's at last "one more sleep" till school begins.

There is a large smile on my face as I walk with my mother in my well-pressed uniform, making my way through the school gates, gaily waving at everyone. The bell rings, signalling school is to begin, and I'm in such a rush that I don't say good-bye to my mother as I run into the classroom, where I pick a seat at the front of the class.

Once everyone is seated, the teacher walks to the blackboard and writes her name.

"I'm Mrs. Campbell," she announces. "I'll be your teacher, and I know most of you can't read what I wrote on the blackboard. That's why I'm not going to erase the words I've written until you can. But I promise you, by the end of the year you'll all be able to write and read your name."

There's a large smile on my face. I'm excited by her words.

"Now, I want everyone in the class to stand up and tell me your name."

One by one, all of us in the class get up from our seat when it's our turn and tell her our name. Once we finish, Mrs. Campbell smiles and announces she will read a story. I am six years old. This is the moment I've dreamt about since I began sitting in my mother's lap looking at the pictures in books. I am convinced this is the most important point in my life. I want to know if the words in books sound like the beautiful voice I hear in my head. I sit still in my seat, like a doll, impatiently waiting for her to read. Finally, Mrs. Campbell opens the book and speaks. Her voice is unlike anything I've imagined—she drones the story in a flat monotone that makes the tale sound dull and dreary. On my first day at school that melodic sound in my head is silenced by my teacher's painful, anguished drawl.

While she speaks, the sun becomes obscured by a cloud and the room feels dark, the animals lose their magic, the castles are now hovels and the people are no longer immortal. From the sound of her voice, I know my toys don't come to life at night. By the time Mrs. Campbell finishes reading, I am so upset I don't hear anything else she says for the rest of the day. When I get home, I lie listlessly on my bed. My sense of disappointment is so deep I can't play with my friends, and I retreat to my room, where I become a doll—lifeless, devoid of blood and tissue. My mood changes. I am no longer a child who makes up stories, but one who refuses to look at a book.

My mother notices my strange behaviour and asks, "Why you stop reading?"

"My teacher read a story and she made it sound bad bad bad."

"How did she do that?"

"Her voice sounded like a dog when it's hit by a car, and I can't get that horrible wail out of my head."

"Kai, listen, and listen up good. If you love something, never let nobody take it from you. Long before she read to you, you loved stories and were always making one up. All these people around here say my child isn't right 'cause she prefer reading to playing, but I tell them to mind them business 'cause at least I didn't make a dunce child. This is what I think: If you don't like what you hear, just make up your own story like you've been doing all your life."

On that day, I make a vow to keep the beautiful story-telling voice alive in my mind, no matter what. While my friends play hopscotch and marbles, I write stories because I know I have to make sure I never sound like Mrs. Campbell. At school, I take painstaking care to learn the alphabet. I am my teacher's star pupil, since I get an "A" in all subjects.

Confident of my academic abilities, I proudly tell my mother I will read her a fairy tale. She smiles when I open the book. I read the story of a sleeping beauty who takes a bite from an apple that puts her into such a deep sleep she can't be woken until a prince kisses her.

As I finish, I innocently ask her with a big smile, "Do you like it?"

When I look at her face, she doesn't look like herself and she's not saying anything. From the way her face twists and turns, I'm not sure what to think and am unprepared for what comes out of her mouth.

"That's not real life," she announces. "I've never heard of anybody's life turning out like that. Come, I'm taking you to the countryside to a place where there are real stories."

My mother grabs my hand and I blindly follow. With her slender frame and ample bottom, she turns a lot of heads. This day is no different. She ignores the stares and comments. Unlike most women, who either press or straighten their hair, she wears hers in a short afro. Sometimes people call it nasty names like "man head."

But no one can ever think she's a man, for this style
accentuates her smooth complexion and high cheekbones.
I'm fearful of asking her why she can't tell me this
story. We walk until we reach the bus station, where she
grabs my hand, and we board a bus headed to the other
side of the island. It's crowded and I'm so uncomfortable.
Occasionally looking out the window, I notice how the
landscape changes as we leave the congestion of town.
There are open fields with brightly coloured flamboyant
trees and coconut trees gently blowing in the wind.
Homes are painted strong blues and yellows, and cows
seem to be languidly ambling everywhere. When we get
to the middle of the island, my mother touches my arm
and tells me we're getting off.

I'm not familiar with this part of Antigua and my mother
securely steers me to the side of the motorway. The pace is
slow enough for me to see a mango tree with a small fruit
on it, and I smile quietly because this tells me that the
season is several weeks away.

Suddenly we turn onto a narrow, unpaved road that
meanders up a hill. After we pass a few houses, the road
narrows further, turning into a footpath. Large mahogany
trees line the path, and the longer we walk on it, the more
the trees appear to get larger. I believe my imagination is
playing tricks on me as I see faces in them. The incline
becomes steeper, and the area feels desolate; my mother
and I are the only persons around. There is nothing and

no one near us. As the hill gets steeper, I hold onto my mother's hand and she pulls me up. Finally, we reach the top. Below us lies the intoxicating greenery of the island, and I'm stunned to see how the hills all slope gently into each other. My mother stands for a moment and stares. Then she sits down under one of those beautiful trees. I sit next to her.

"Where's this?" I finally ask.

"I'm sure they never talk about this place at your school," she replies. There is silence for a while before she continues. "Here is so full of stories."

"The teacher says the only historic place on the island is Nelson's Dockyard," I answer.

"Kai, there is so much more out there. There is plenty to say about what happened in the past, but no one cares to remember. It's so sad. This place is called Montula."

The word "Montula" sounds foreign; it is unlike anything I've heard before. I repeat it and it seems to leave an echo in the air. A breeze blows and I think I hear it whisper the word back at me.

My mother sits up. She looks me directly in the eye. "Have they told you about Montula at school?"

"No," I say. "I've never heard about it." Then I repeat the word again. Once more it echoes in the wind. I look at my mother, who doesn't seem to hear it as she just stares at the field.

"I'm going to tell you a story. Long ago, they chained people and brought them across the ocean to work. They worked till they dropped dead, and then were buried in unmarked graves."

There's a long silence before I exclaim, "Mammie, that's a horrible story."

"Kai, I didn't make it up. This is real life. But here at Montula it was different. This is the resting place for the slaves, and this was where they finally found peace. It sad that no one even remember this place is here or this story."

She continues to look at the sloping hillside, lost in her own thoughts, and that's when I hear the Ancestors clearly for the first time. It's the echo I've been hearing since I started walking up the hill. Their voice comes to me in thousands of whispers and I sit up in shock. I look around. There are only two people sitting on this hill, my mother and me; there is no one else around. No radio. No phone. Nothing. It is in this moment that the Ancestors realize I can hear them, because suddenly they become one distinct voice that tells me I'm sitting in the graveyard of the forgotten people.

Most children would be scared and run from that place, but not me. I'm a storyteller. I didn't feel a desire to flee in fear. This is what my imagination is made from. My mother brought me here because she said there were stories I need to know, and I believe they are going to tell me those tales. When they ask if I'm afraid, I shake my head, knowing I cannot speak with my mother next to me.

They tell me their voices can be heard all over the island, but not by everyone. That's when they instruct me to bend my head into the wind and I will hear them even more clearly. Looking at the rolling hills, my mother doesn't notice how strange I'm acting, and I'm unsure if she also hears the voices. As if they can read my mind, they tell me she can't and warn me to keep this a secret. I bend my ear into the wind, their voice becoming much clearer. I hear each word and syllable. Then they whisper their first story.

On the way home, as the crowded bus zooms into town, I'm squeezed into a small space, but I don't care as I bend my head into the wind. The voices whisper stories unlike any I've ever heard, much more interesting than Snow White. By the time I'm home, I realize I don't need to read a book. I take up my pen and start to write their stories.

Each night, I listen to the Ancestors before the sun goes down. My mother sees me with my pad and paper, scribbling words, and rightly assumes I am happily writing a story. I tell no one of them. They are my secret.

In grade five, I read out loud one of my stories to the class. In this tale, I wrote about a woman buried at Montula. I did not describe her short, unhappy life; instead I tell them that she cries when people walk on her grave and don't know it's her resting place. She sees young lovers kissing and children playing. From her grave, she finally feels happiness, something she never knew. All the girls in my class are in tears when I finish, but my teacher stares at me incredulously, as if I am a demon, and then

she tells me my words are blasphemous because spirits
don't talk and my story must be the work of the devil.
But I don't care that it's different from what everyone else
in the class reads. Their plots are all the same. They read
like this: "I go to the market with my mother to buy fish.
The prince is passing by in a carriage. When he sees me,
he thinks I am the most beautiful woman in the land.
He stops his carriage and tells me to hop in. As we ride
around the land, he falls in love with me."

I strut around the schoolyard, believing in my
uniqueness despite the confines of my pleated, beige
uniform. I'm surrounded by other little girls like myself,
with dark brown skin and short tightly curled hair—
fatherless and poor—but I stand apart because I always
get the top grade in class and my vivid imagination
unleashes stories.

My teachers wear their pressed hair in severe buns.
They carry canes and use them freely on those kids who
answer incorrectly or in a disrespectful tone. I am being
taught not to question; my voice must always sound
deferential. It's like they want to stifle who I am, but none
of my teachers are aware of my storytelling voice that
can't be silenced.

At this point, everything around me, from my homelife
to the way my mind thinks, is contrary to the world
around me. Although I live with my mother, another
person lives in our house, and that person is not a man.
Her name is Vee, and she shares the same bed as my

mother. They also hold hands and smile into each other's eyes. I see their lips brush tenderly against each other's every morning.

Their togetherness is the cause of a major scandal on this small island, where anything out of the ordinary is strongly condemned. On Sundays, the island takes a break from life to head to church. Preachers stand on a pulpit and rage at sinners. They preach that the Bible sanctions that only men and women should live together; no other union is acceptable. No church will open its door to us.

We aren't invited out often. Two of my uncles stopped talking to my mother because they believe she is the world's biggest sinner and will go straight to hell because of her love for a woman. These two men have fathered children with different women outside of wedlock, but they never think their actions are wrong, even though their actions are not sanctioned by the Bible. The rest of her brothers are indifferent or pretend to be. Still, they never visit us, and they rarely drop off their children to play with me. I know nothing of Vee's family—not whether she has a brother or sister, not what her parents look like. The only thing I know is that she grew up on another island.

People yell horrible things whenever my mother walks on the streets:

"Woman, you went crazy after that man leave you."

"You're not the first woman that a man treat bad. The list long long long."

"God going to strike you down one day for all your sins. You are a sick woman."

I don't understand the hatred towards her and Vee. I see two women who truly care for each other. It's an understanding that goes so deep they easily finish each other's sentences. Many of my friends tell me their parents raise their voices at each other and quarrel over silly things like not enough salt in the rice, but I never knew anything like this, because my mother and Vee always spoke gently to each other. Each month, my mother has severe cramps from her menstrual cycle, and Vee lies with her on the bed, massaging her tummy. I peek at them as they lie together, two forms so close together they look like a statue of one. Their relationship is unlike any fairy tale I've read. It is a story that has never been penned—the words without form or plan. It just is.

While my mother cleans and cooks for a family in one of the rich areas of the island, Vee works in a store owned by a Syrian. Neither of them wants me to cook and clean for another. They love to bake, and in order to make extra money, they spend hours baking and decorating cakes. As I progress through school, I discover that Vee is more educated than my mother: she confides that her father removed her from school before she took her final exams but doesn't explain why. She spends many nights patiently helping me with my schoolwork, urging me to be my best.

When I am in grade five, my academic abilities make me eligible to sit for the exam for a scholarship to the most prestigious girls' school on the island for my secondary education.

I plead with my mother and Vee: "Mammie, I want this so bad bad bad. Please let me write the exam this year. I so believe I can win."

"Kai, just wait a year when you're more grown up and can handle it better if you win or lose."

I reply before thinking. "I want to have a better life than what we have. This will make it happen faster."

We are poor. Although painted bright yellow with green shutters, our house is very small. Seven small steps can take you from the living room to our balcony, and we spend a lot of our time outside sitting on the gallery. Inside, the rooms are divided by thin wooden partitions that don't touch the roof. It's easy to hear what everyone says. There are no ornaments on our walls other than the peeling paint. Our water comes from the communal pipe on the road. When it rains, we place numerous tin cans around the house to collect the water that drips through holes in the roof. We even have an old fridge that never keeps a drink cold.

After I speak, my mother looks around the house and says, "Write the exam, Kai. We only want the best for you."

The exam is in a stone building—made from large blocks— whose walls are overgrown with vines. It is an old structure constructed under British rule. Judged by its size and shape, it was an important facility in its time. But on that day it is the structure in which a consequential exam will take place.

Inside, the temperature is several degrees cooler because of the trees. The desks are arranged in rows of five. A lady in a severe black skirt and a starched white shirt asks my name. There is nothing welcoming in her manner; neither are there words of encouragement from her lips. Despite my nervousness, I speak calmly and she checks my name off the list. She does not smile when she points to a seat.

I don't recognize the faces of any of the girls already seated. In their nervousness, they are fanning themselves with scrap paper, although the room is not hot. At ten minutes to ten, the woman gets up from her desk and hands out an exam to all participants. Her harsh voice instructs everyone to turn over their paper when the bell rings; we will have three hours to write. The breeze blows softly through the shutters, allowing the air to caress my skin. Trees continue to shade the building, maintaining the cool respite, but I don't have time to ponder any of my thoughts. As the bell rings everyone's head diligently bends over their desk; I hesitate before I start the exam; I bend my ear into the wind, hearing the Ancestors' voice, and then I write as if my life depends on it.

A few weeks later, the headmistress calls me into her office and I nervously go. To my surprise, my mother and Vee are there. Unsure what to expect, I sit uncomfortably next to them, wondering if I've done something wrong.

The headmistress sees my nervousness and smiles brightly, reassuring me everything is fine.

"Kai, you made this school proud," she announces. "I'm so happy to tell you that you've won the scholarship. You beat sixty other girls on the island, most of them in grade six. You've been one of the brightest girls I've taught and I'm very happy for you. This scholarship will pay for your books, uniform and tuition until you reach form five. Your entire secondary education is paid for if you maintain your grades. You are the first girl from this school to win."

My mother shouts, "Kai, you win. I'm so happy, happy, happy!" Then she gets up and hugs me so tightly that I can't breathe. Vee also joins my mother, jumping up from her seat and shaking me. 'You win, Kai. You really and truly win. You beat all of them. I always knew that you could do it. I'm too proud of you."

The headmistress clears her throat. "Now, let's calm down. We're all proud of Kai. And the judging committee was so impressed with Kai's writing abilities that one of the judges, the owner of the newspaper, will be publishing her essay in the Saturday paper. Congratulations, Kai, you now have your first published article. You're on your way to becoming a writer."

Early the following Saturday morning before the sun rises, I look up from my sleep to see my mother and Vee standing over me, waving the newspaper, and I remember that my article is in it. Excitedly, I wipe the sleep from my eyes and sit up. My eyes grow wide with pride as I look at my article in print, and the biggest smile I've ever known spreads over my face. All three of us crowd onto my small bed as I read. The article was my answer to the question, What will you do with your education?

Every night my mother sits next to me and encourages me to be the best. She taught me a rhyme: "Good, better, best. Never let it rest. Until we make our good better and our better best." My mother wants me to be the best because she never had that chance. She never learned to read. She told me that learning is the greatest gift available, and if we have a chance we should never stop.

When I told my mother that my grades made me eligible to apply for the scholarship, she wept with glee. She told me this is the best school on the island, it will give me the best chance in life. Then, she confided that I am the first woman in our family who can read.

My mother whispered to me why she never learned to read. Her story was not a nice story. When she spoke, she held her head low with shame. My mother's disgrace made me vow that one day I'd write a story that'd make her a heroine.

As a small child, my mother and I walked on the road and came across a tall fence. She told me that in life we all must learn to scale high walls. I thought she wanted me to climb over the wall and I began to do this, but the wall was smooth. I couldn't find any grooves to scale it. She watched my desperation, and when I cried from failure, she told me that in her world there is a wall built high up to the sky. It looks like it reaches heaven. She has tried to scale it. Although she looks for the cracks and grooves, all she feels is a smooth surface.

On the day she gave birth to me, she declared

that I will climb that wall and that was why

she gave me the only thing that she knew

would prepare me for life: a book. She said,

"This will teach you there are no walls."

My mother is a maid. She's spent years clean-

ing the homes of people much richer than us.

These people read books for learning and lei-

sure. She saw their children doing homework

and wanted me to have that chance. When I

was stuck on my homework, I could never ask

her to help; she couldn't. She advised me that

I'd have to learn everything on my own—as

much as she wishes, she can't help me.

My mother stared at me whenever I wrote

words. Her eyes held a look of wonderment

and curiosity. She'd take in every stroke of the

pen. One day, I caught her with a pen in her

hand, awkwardly trying to form the letters.

As she tried to balance the pen and find a comfortable position to use it in, I went over and put my hand on top of hers. Together we formed the alphabet letters. Then when she mastered her letters, I taught her to write her name.

If I win this scholarship, I will make my mother proud. I will continue to strive to be the best and increase my vocabulary. Once I graduate, there are two things I wish to accomplish. I want to continue to teach adults and children who, like my mother, never had the opportunity to learn to read or write. But I also love stories and enjoy writing them, and that's why I want to become a writer. The stories of the people I have known deserve to be told.

In our little house, the words of my article hang in the air. Then we hear the neighbours and others moving on the streets. My mother looks at the clock. She mutters that she has to leave. Vee also has to work. I'm upset because I want this moment to linger. I want to read to them again. Why don't they have more time to enjoy my words? The sun rises. The clock ticks. They are now late for work. Later, when I became an adult, they told me that although this was one of the happiest moments of their lives, they resented that they didn't have time to savour it. Before they leave, they promise we'll celebrate that evening. When they get home from work, my mother and Vee tell me to stay away from the kitchen, they are baking a surprise. They happily bustle around the kitchen, making preparations. Soon the smell of a freshly baked cake wafts through the air and my mouth waters. They see I am excited and tell me to be patient, they have a really big surprise. I go outside, and to keep calm I bend my ear into the wind.

In the early evening, my mother and Vee call me to come inside, where sitting on our dining table is a cake that looks like a book. The cover design is a girl who looks like me, seated on the steps of our home, reading a book. I burst into tears of joy. I don't want to cut my cake—I want it to last forever—but they tell me it's meant to be eaten. We sit on the balcony and eat. The Ancestors are there, but they aren't whispering a story.

"Kai, you make me proud," my mother says. "Your story reminded me that we have to keep climbing the wall. For some time Vee and I been talking about opening a store and selling cakes. We already get orders, and Vee knows how to decorate them because her grandmother taught her. You're not going to start your new school saying your mother is a maid."

CHAPTER TWO

Saturdays

On the morning of my first day at my new secondary school, I awake very early. The small hand of the clock is at five and the large at six. Electricity is off—in the semi-dark I make my way to the bathroom. I light a candle and bathe in darkness; on the wall I see the shadow of a girl not yet a woman. This image, a subtle likeness of me, portrays nothing. It doesn't say if I am scared or confident; this shadow doesn't reveal any of my thoughts.

With the house still in darkness, I return to my bedroom, where my school uniform is waiting on a hanger. There are still a few hours before classes begin, but I'm so excited I impulsively put on the uniform. The dress feels silky as it easily slides onto my body. I stand in front of the mirror; my reflection excites me, and in my exuberance I twirl. The skirt floats high. The crisp pleats move up and down, rising and falling as if a gentle breeze is buoying it. I keep turning around in circles until I get dizzy and the room spins. When I stop, my pleats all gently return to their correct position, as if I'd never whirled.

I go outside to speak with the Ancestors, knowing their stories will calm me. As I bend my head into the wind, their voice floats to me. I expect them to tell me a tale of life before I was born, but instead they remind me that not many of my forebearers knew how to read.

As I sit on the balcony of my house, with the glorious pink sunrise above, I ponder their words. Six years have passed since I began bending my ear into the wind. I am no longer a small child: my feet are larger, my limbs longer and stronger; my body has new curves and shape; even my face has lost its childish shape, and a very attractive reflection blossoms. Despite my changes, our existence is so intertwined—a bond as strong as a mother cradling her child—that I can't imagine my life without them. I write their words on paper: story after story of the forgotten people who once lived on this island. But on this morning their words surprise me, when they repeat that I am one of the few who hear their voice as it blows in the breeze and reveal that from the moment of my birth they were waiting for me to hear them.

There is movement inside the house. My mother is up and I go inside. She smiles when she sees me. "Kai, you look all grown up in that uniform." She quickly turns her head and I see her tear-filled eyes.

I don't respond, because I can't find my voice.

"Are you excited?" she asks after she wipes her eyes.

I nod. Words still elude me.

She pats me on my head, assuring me, "Things will be fine, Kai. Trust me. The new isn't always easy, 'cause we don't know what will happen next."

My new school is not at all like my old school. It's more than the imposing gates that have the school logo emblazed on it. I watch the cars glide through the gates, dropping off the students, with total fascination. At my old school the kids either walked or took a bus; no one knew this kind of luxury. This is an all-girls' school. The students who step out of the cars look and act different, and they don't speak patois; everyone talks in the refined singsong accent that I hear whenever I am in the bank with my mother.

At my old school, most of the students are like me, the colour of a rich chocolate cake, but here the students come in different skin tones—from deep ebony to shades of honey.

The school bell rings, signaling the beginning of the year, and I make my way to class. It's in pristine condition, from the clean blackboard to the sturdiness of my desk. Everything looks perfect. For the past two years I sat at a broken desk, and my mother was constantly removing splinters from my fingers.

I don't know anyone. Several of the girls stare at me but don't say anything. The teacher enters and writes her name on the blackboard. "I know most of you know each other," she begins, "but there are a few new faces. I want everyone to stand up and introduce themselves."

At my turn, I stand up and firmly announce, "Kai Robbins."

The teacher interrupts, "You're the girl who won the scholarship. I read your essay in the paper; it was excellent. And I also spoke with your former headmistress. She had great things to say about you. Welcome to your new school. Everyone, please take the time to introduce yourself to Kai. Why don't you tell us something about yourself?"

I'm so nervous that I speak in a broken dialect, "Me a come here from—"

There is loud, explosive laughter.

"Kai, you can't speak like that in this school," the teacher reproaches me. "And talking Patois is not acceptable at any time. You are only to speak proper English at school. That's been the problem we've had with you scholarship girls: you don't know how to speak properly."

"Yes, Ma'am," I reply, ashamed and battered.

As I ease into my seat twenty-two pairs of eyes peer at me as if I don't belong. In the background, I hear snickering. I soon learn that this introduction gave me the nickname "scholarship girl", an embarrassing moniker repeated year after year amongst several of my classmates whenever they wanted to remind me I was not one of them.

At recess, my classmates openly exclude me from their cliques and conversations because I am the scholarship girl. By the end of the first day I walk home, feeling very dejected. That's when I make a decision to learn to speak better English so that no one will laugh at me. Phrases like "me nah know" and "me nah do um" are eliminated from my vocabulary.

When I get home, my mother and Vee want to hear about my day, but I am quiet. At dinner they look imploringly at me.

"It nah go well," I finally confide. "I mean, it didn't go well."

"Give it time," Vee says. "Those girls may be stuck up, but they can't change that you're there. They have no other choice than to accept you."

"Kai, don't worry about them. You there to learn, and that's all that matters," my mother adds.

The first day merges into day two and then into day three. Nothing changes. I remain alone. During recess, I find a secluded corner and pass time until one of my classmates, Brittany, follows me.

Her first words are surprising, "Kai, do you have a boyfriend?"

"Why do you want to know? Is it because you want to

carry back news to the other girls about the
scholarship girl."

"No. You're here alone, so I came to talk with you. I
thought that was a good conversation starter. The girls in
our class have an attitude problem. And if it makes you
feel better, you're not the only one they've treated like
that. I was once their target."

"Really? Why?"

"When I moved here from Trinidad, I was an outsider
like you. My dad is from there, while my mom is from
Antigua, so we lived in Trinidad for several years. I
learned to stand up to them. My dad's a judge and he told
me what to say. It scared them and they kept away." She
laughs as she speaks, and I quickly forget that I don't want
to like anyone at school.

"Hey, I have a thick skin," I reply. "I have to where I
come from."

"Let's forget about them. So are you going to answer
my question? Do you have a boyfriend?"

"No," I respond firmly. "I don't really like boys. Do you
like them?"

"Of course I do. Who doesn't?" She smiles, believing
there is no other way. Then, when she sees my surprise,
she laughs. Her laugh is hearty and contagious, and I find
myself warming to her infectious happiness. "It'll happen
one day to you. It happens to everyone. The boy I like
doesn't really notice me. But he's so cute! And I really like
him. Maybe one day he'll realize I'm the one for him."

I can't imagine anyone not noticing her. Brittany is gorgeous, with her thick, wavy hair that she wears in a long ponytail hanging halfway down her back. Her skin is brown, like a milk chocolate bar, and it appears as smooth. I have this urge to touch her to see if it feels as silky as it looks.

We become friends for all the wrong reasons, and in the strange twist of life, we are inseparable. Most importantly, Brittany never calls me "scholarship girl." Brittany talks about boys a lot, and I enjoy her breezy chatter. It doesn't matter that we are on different ends of the spectrum. She likes me because I'm serious. Although she is a bit obsessed with boys, I enjoy listening to her changing crushes, but I have nothing to contribute to those conversations for several years.

I believe I am immune to boys. It is more than my chatter with Brittany. It is all around me. As I progress through school, I'm the only person who doesn't talk about boys. By the time I'm fifteen, the girls at school have boyfriends and crushes. Even the girls in my neighbourhood are also going through this same phase. For a long time, I look at boys and wonder what is so great about the opposite sex. I only know a household with two women loving each other. I witness their love and partnership. With no interest in boys, I wonder if I would choose a woman. I realize differently on a scorching August day.

It is really hot—more so than usual because everyone walks around fanning themselves with paper or wiping perspiration from their skin with handkerchiefs. The focal point of all conversations centers on the same theme: no one remembers a time when the breeze hasn't blown for days. In this heat, my mother sends me to a faraway store to pick up some item that she can't get close to home. By the time I reach the store, I'm dripping with sweat. And inside, the temperature is several degrees cooler. Immediately, I feel refreshed. To elongate this cool respite, I walk the neat aisles.

As I make my way around the store, a young man walks past me, and for the first time in my life, I feel the overwhelming urge to look at a member of the opposite sex. He is over six feet tall, with skin that appears as if the sun spent hours kissing his flesh, resulting in a bronzed hue. I look at my dark skin and compare it to his—we're like a contrast of black and gold. On this island, we call lighter-skin people like him "red." Then he turns and his eyes stare at me; his eyes are unlike anything I've ever seen—they are the colour of the sea when it glistens in the midday sun. His jeans hug his legs, and his shirt hangs loosely from his shoulders. He walks with an air of authority. For some unknown reason I feel my heart race. Someone at the counter calls, "Hayden."

Turning around to answer, he moves to stand behind the cash register. I blindly follow him, loitering next to the cash register to keep him within eyesight as I pretend to rummage through the goods. Noticing me hovering, he asks if I need help. Terribly embarrassed, I run out of the store without buying what my mother needs.

I think about him all the time. Each time I walk past the store, I hope to see him. Occasionally he's walking on the street and my heart races; it feels like it will jump out of my body. One day, as I'm standing outside the store, talking with my mother's friend, a nosey woman who sells food on the side of the road, Hayden appears. In mid-sentence I stop speaking and watch him walk to his car. He has a tennis racquet under his arm. His white shorts and shirt cling to his frame, creating a strong, masculine appearance. I let out a deep sigh as I take all of him in; I think he is the most handsome man alive. When he gets to his car door, he fumbles in his pockets; his keys aren't there and he gets aggravated. Finally, smiling to himself with relief, he finds them. He quickly opens the door and slips into the seat. I hear his engine turn as the car springs to life and Hayden drives away.

My mother's friend's voice is harsh: "You can't have a man like him." Her words shock me, and I snap out of my euphoria. "He from a good family and people like them don't know we exist."

Without responding, I look down uncomfortably at my shoes. They are old and worn. My clothing isn't much better, and immediately I'm aware of the difference between us. It's the wall I face each day at school. This recognition is like a strap hitting my back. The sting brings tears to my eyes. As I try to hold them back my mother's friend notices my distress. She grabs one of my

hands and holds it tightly. With her free hand, she begins
to place some tamarind stew in a small cup but stops.

"Better not give you this 'cause it's not sweet, and you
don't need any more bitterness to manage." She rustles
around her tray, grabbing a chocolate bar and handing it
to me. "Here," she says, "this sweet and easy on your
taste buds."

"Thanks," I reply but I'm not interested in eating.

"Kai, you prettier than a picture and I'm not lying
about that. I see the boys in our neighbourhood trying
to get your attention, but you always turn your head the
other way. I know they are a botheration, but not all of
them are bad—some just pretend to be. Men must always
look like they're the boss. You're young and waiting for
the special boy, and that's good. Right now, what you have
is a schoolgirl crush. As women, we think about a prince,
and I guess that red-skinned boy is your prince. Listen
here, a good boy will turn up at your door one day. Just
don't expect him to be that red boy."

I continue to stare down the road, wondering how it'll
feel to sit in the car with Hayden.

I never tell Brittany about my crush. I keep my fantasy
about the golden-coloured boy with aqua eyes to myself.
Not only am I fearful she will laugh at me, but also,
deep down inside, I secretly know that she, with her
good family background, is the type of girl someone like
him is interested in. I spend many hours and months
daydreaming about the six-foot boy named Hayden.

Although I keep my daydreams to myself, Brittany eventually discovers them.

One Saturday afternoon, while I'm working at my mother's cake store, Brittany and her mom walk through the door. This is the first time I'm meeting her mother, and I stare hard because she's so light in complexion that if I hadn't known her family origin, I'd easily assume she has full European ancestry. Her light skin is further complemented by her grey eyes. She sees me staring, and I apologize: "I'm sorry to be staring at you. It's just that . . . well, you don't look like what I expected."

She laughs good-naturedly. "I think God played a sick joke on me and forgot that I need melanin because I live in the Caribbean. But then everyone will say, if they ever question your background, turn around, you're blessed with the nicest, roundest bottom."

She proudly displays her ample *derrière*. "I think this is what keeps my husband happy."

Brittany rolls her eyes into the sky, while my mother and Vee chuckle in amusement. She speaks to my mother and Vee about the cakes. "Brittany keeps telling me that I should buy your cakes for my tea parties and now I know why. They not only look good, but they sure smell divine. I need one for my bridge party this afternoon. Every time I have to host the bridge party, my friends never eat my desserts. My helper is excellent, but she can't figure out how to make anything sweet to save her life. Not even my sugar-loving husband eats her cakes. She just doesn't understand that when you have tea parties, you need a good dessert."

Brittany and I huddle in a corner and chat, ignoring the adult conversation. Through the corner of her eyes, her mother sees us and smiles. She looks at my mother. "What's Kai doing this afternoon? Does she have any plans?"

I shake my head.

"If your mother doesn't mind, why doesn't Kai spend the rest of the afternoon with Brittany? I'm hosting a bridge party. And I know my daughter hates hanging out in the house with a bunch of old women."

"Mom, please, can I go? Please please please."

My mom and Vee exchange looks. They know they can't win this one. Vee smiles. "Kai, you go and enjoy yourself. We don't need you this afternoon."

"Thanks. I'll bring her back early this evening. But I didn't come here to get your daughter. I need a wonderful cake. I just want to beat my sister-in-law, Catherine. She's so haughty. I can't wait to see her look of shock because I have a very divine dessert." She points to the chocolate cake. "I'll get that one. I don't know a woman who can say no to chocolate."

Brittany's home is vastly different from mine. I live in a neighbourhood where small, brightly coloured wooden homes are huddled close together, while Brittany's is a large, concrete home with an impeccable manicured lawn. Inside, all the rooms are spacious with high ceilings. The

large living room is formal, yet relaxing. All I can think is
that her home transports me to another country because
it's like a picture from a foreign magazine.

I'm so awed by her pretty home that I blindly follow
her mother to the kitchen, where she hands the maid the
cake, instructing her how to cut it. Not sounding dispar-
aging or dictatorial, she does this with ease and grace—
making it appear like a natural event. Silently I remember
that once, before they opened the store, my mother was
the one taking these orders.

Brittany gleefully guides me through her home,
holding my hand. That afternoon, I glimpse a world
I never knew existed. We go with her mother to her
spacious bedroom, where we excitedly watch her dress
for her bridge party. She takes out several outfits from
her cupboard and asks our opinions as she tries them on.
She enjoys our "oohs" and "ahhs" as we either approve or
disapprove. Finally, she chooses something to wear and
tells us to leave her alone. We go to the balcony, where
Brittany tells me that it's fun to watch her mother's
friends arrive in their bright, beautiful fashionable attire.

The first person to arrive looks at Brittany. "How is
my niece?"

"I'm fine, Aunt Catherine," Brittany politely responds.

As she walks away, her aunt looks at me, then turns to
her friend, observing, "I don't know how my sister-in-law
allows Brittany to associate with the maid's daughter."

Brittany loses her smile and just glares at her aunt's
back. She doesn't say anything as she grabs my hand,

taking me to her room, where she rummages through her cupboard. Without looking at me, she hands me a dress. "Put this on," she instructs. "I hardly wear it and it'll look good on you."

I hesitate for a moment, but seeing the sincerity in her eyes, I quietly step into Brittany's beautiful blue dress. She smiles. "You look amazing!"

I turn to look at myself and can't believe how the dress has transformed me. For several minutes I just stare. Then Brittany hands me a bag filled with clothes.

"Here, take these with you. I don't wear them, and with your beautiful figure, you'll look fantastic in them."

My eyes fill up with water. "You don't have to."

Brittany replies, "Let's not mention this again. It's our secret."

We go back outside. As the rest of the women arrive, they smile and call out to Brittany. They look curiously at me, and one or two women ask who I am. Brittany always says, "My best friend. She's the smartest woman in the world."

On the following Saturday, Brittany and her mother are once again at the shop.

"That cake was the toast of my bridge party," Brittany's mother gushes. "You should have seen how my sister-in-law, Catherine, was upset because everyone raved about it. I don't normally host two parties in a row, but a friend who was supposed to host this week got sick. Is Kai doing anything? She's welcome to come over."

That's how I started going to Brittany's every Saturday afternoon. Some weeks there are bridge parties, but it doesn't matter to Brittany and me because we always find something fun to do. While her mother has a busy social life, her father spends most Saturday afternoons sitting on the balcony, reading a book. A short, muscular man, he smiles as his wife busies herself around the house. He enjoys joining Brittany and me on the balcony, where we always find something to talk about. I learn that he grew up in the Trinidadian countryside, and like me, he also won a scholarship to his secondary school—the first of many scholarships he won, all leading to his career in law.

An intellect with strong Caribbean roots, he is very supportive of my writing and always asks me to read my stories. Sitting on his balcony, with a soft breeze touching our skin, he becomes my mentor as he guides me with tips to improve my writing. His words are always the same: "Kai, follow your heart and you'll become who you are meant to be."

On the Saturday that changes my life, I am with Brittany in her room when I hear a car horn. Her mother calls, "Brittany, your cousin is here to see you."

An elated Brittany jumps up with delight and tells me her favourite cousin promised to visit—she hadn't seen him in a while. Then she whispers, "I didn't really expect him to come. He keeps saying he will but never does."

I follow her to the living room, and there, sitting on her couch, is the aqua-eyed boy, looking as strikingly handsome as ever. My mouth drops open; I can't move my legs as I stare at him in shock.

Brittany pokes me when she sees my reaction to him and says, "Hayden sure is cute."

I hide behind her as she introduces us. My heart is fluctuating wildly, and it feels as if the room is spinning. I'm wholly aware of him and nothing else. His shirt is clinging to his body from sweat. I quickly learn that he just left the tennis court. I make out his muscular arms and chest. He is lean and his legs slope seductively down from his hips. Up close, his aqua eyes are even more mesmerizing, and they're all I can look at. I can't do anything but stare at him.

Brittany is amused by my reaction, and she also notices that Hayden is looking intently at me.

He smiles. "I see your friend sometimes when she comes into Daddy's store." He laughs adding, "We've never officially met."

I want to disappear into the ground as I remember running out of the store.

"I saw you when you came to our store on a really hot day. You were loafing around the aisles."

"Yes," I mumble, wishing I could leave the room. "I remember seeing you."

"Wow, this is interesting," Brittany interjects.

"Brittany, you know I'm going to spend the rest of the afternoon with you and your cute friend."

I slowly begin to lose my nervousness. Hayden asks me several questions, which I answer. I relax and begin to speak freely. He responds to my voice. I learn that he is quick-witted and likes to bandy words about. Despite his appearance, he is as serious as I am, and we have a similar sense of humour.

Brittany brags that I won the scholarship to the school, and it was my essay that was printed in the paper. Hayden confides that he'd read it and was impressed with the writer. To my surprise, I discover he is an avid reader. As we talk, it seems as if Brittany disappears. Eventually, she leaves us alone, but we don't notice when she does. The afternoon drifts into early evening. Hayden looks deeply into my eyes as he's leaving and says, "I hope to see you again."

Brittany appears from nowhere, replying, "Kai spends every Saturday with me."

After he leaves, there is a hushed silence. Then Brittany and I fall onto the couch, giggling.

"I was waiting," she says when she controls herself. "I knew at some point you had to notice someone." And we look at each other and giggle some more.

The following Saturday, Hayden calls Brittany to see if I'm there. Once Brittany says yes, he tells her he'll be right there. This becomes his routine. Brittany teases me that Hayden never visited so often and now he does because of me. I am afraid to believe her. Whatever walls existed, they crumble, as I notice Hayden's eyes are alight whenever I'm in the room. Eventually, he lets down his guard and flirts outright with me. I respond. Brittany sits back in her seat, smiling. Her mother notices the growing

attraction and enjoys watching our blossoming romance.
She snidely tells Brittany, "I can't wait to see the look on
Catherine's face when she learns about this. You know
what a snob she is. This will really kill her."

One Saturday Brittany's mother's car breaks down, and
this leads to a bit of a dilemma because she can't drop me
home. Hayden smiles confidently as he steps in and offers
his assistance. He announces, "Don't worry, Aunt Sonia.
My car is outside and I'll drop Kai home."

Brittany's mother thinks this is an excellent solution,
and that is how I become the girl in Hayden's car.

When I give him the directions to turn onto the road
that leads to my house, I know he's never been to this side
of the world. The island is small, but the roads are built
to avoid areas of extreme poverty, like where I live. Until
that night, Hayden may have driven along the main road,
but he'd never turned onto the side road that leads to my
world. The darkness can't hide the contrast of our lives.
The houses are small and cramped with no yard space.
The roads are filled with potholes, which Hayden skilfully
swerves. Mangy dogs roam the streets. Abandoned tires
and rotten galvanized metal sheeting sit outside. Garbage
is strewn everywhere. People stand on the road, while
others peer through their windows as we drive along.
There are small children playing in the streets in their
underwear. Here, small houses abut each other—the
neighbours fully aware of each other's life. My world is
claustrophobic and crowded, in stark contrast to Hayden's

world. I hold my head down, fearful of his opinion as he learns about Kai outside of his cousin's home.

"So this is where you live," he says when he parks outside the house.

I nod and say, "Thanks for the lift. Your aunt really appreciated your help."

"I'm always happy to help. Kai, do you realize I now know where you live? That means, I can come by anytime."

I hang my head. "It's not much. I guess you'll stop flirting with me."

"Do you think I'm that shallow?"

"I don't, but I wasn't sure how you'd feel about where I live."

"I like you, Kai. Why do you think I come to Brittany's on Saturday afternoon?"

"You mean that it's not because you're bored and don't have any friends?"

He laughs loudly after I speak, and when he controls himself, he replies, "I have lots of friends, believe me. There is an abundance of people. They even tease me about my Saturday-afternoon girlfriend."

I blush.

"I'm not going to pretend. I'm not good at it. The truth is, I enjoy being with you and I can't wait to see you again after we part."

I am afraid to look at him and just keep staring into space.

He sees my shyness and asks, "Will you be at Brittany's birthday party next week?"

I nod.

"Good, that'll give you time to think about what I said." He bends over and softly kisses my cheek, leaving a sweet tingly sensation.

As I watch Hayden drive away, I'm in a world of my own, staring into the distance long after I can no longer see his car. The stars seem reachable. The roads are wider, and I feel like I've scaled another notch on the wall.

"Now I know what you holding out for."

The words catch me by surprise, shaking me from my reverie. At the corner three boys from my neighbourhood, who linger constantly at that spot, are standing under the lamplight. They are part of a group who usually while away their time by passing sarcastic comments at young women. They harass with sexual taunts, and I've been the brunt of many of their remarks. Turning quickly, I make my way into the house because I know these boys are troublemakers and they just saw Hayden dropping me home. Their words reach me before I can close the door.

"Me can show you why a boy like him want you. Me can teach you to ride the horse and keep the rider galloping."

"That school make you think you better than we. But when he done with you, you will come back home for the real thing. Me sure that red boy can't make you scream."

I make my way through the door. And as I turn to close it, jeering at me, the boys grab their crotches.

The moon sits like a giant pearl on a black satin sheet with chips of diamonds the night of Brittany's party. It's early—most of the guests haven't arrived—and I'm drawn to her patio to look up at the sky. My mind is on Hayden; he's all I've thought about all week. I'm busy looking at the constellations when he arrives. He sneaks up from behind, wraps his arms around my waist and presses his body into me. His breath is fast and sweet on my neck.

"What are you doing?" he asks as he spins me around and pulls me to him.

"Counting stars," I reply. My breathing grows rapid because we're standing close to each other. I've never been this intimate with him. I smell his cologne. He smells wonderful and I think it's a very masculine smell.

"There are too many stars to count," he replies in a knowing fashion.

"You only think that if you've never attempted to count them."

"There are billions upon billions of stars. Have you ever counted all of them?"

"No."

"Then don't waste any more time. Dance with me."

Before I can reply, he leads me to the dance floor. The quick rhythm of Soca (Calypso) fades to a slow beat and he pulls me closer. I am aware of his strength as our bodies move. My blood is pumping fast as it rushes through my veins. I am overpowered by this sensation and it leaves me speechless. When the song finishes, I quickly disengage from him and run outside.

My breathing is heavy, and I try to calm myself. I take a few quick breaths. As I stand on the balcony with the breeze touching my skin, I remember the way our bodies moved. I stretch over the balcony to feel the cool breeze.

"Still counting stars?" he asks.

I stare at him—my mouth dry—and cannot find any words.

"I followed you out here after you left me on the dance floor. Don't you know that you can't leave a guy alone after a few dances—it makes him look bad? You're not good for my reputation."

"Sorry, Hayden, I didn't mean it that way."

"I know. Do you mind if we continue dancing?"

I nod and we return inside. The lights are dim. The moon's rays float into the room and sit on us. I try to find something to say but can't. I'm aware of one emotion: Hayden is next to me and this is not a dream.

"I've been waiting for the right time to talk. I came early tonight because I want to spend as much time as possible with you."

Without thinking, I blurt out, "I'm glad because that's exactly what I want."

We know we are both thinking the same thing and don't feel a need to express ourselves further. The music continues and we stay close together—our bodies always touching—aware of the world that is opening for us.

The moon is bright and we both stare at it from the dance floor. We talk and we laugh. The walls crumble as we explore our attraction. I feel compelled to stay with

him, once he wants to be with me. Drifting onto the
balcony, we stand facing each other. I smile and he smiles
back. He touches my hand and I feel his strength. I put
both my hands in his.
I've never experienced anything like what I'm feeling.
A shy smile covers my face. His height doesn't feel
imposing, though he is taller than me. His hypnotic eyes,
so different from my own, mesmerize me. I know he
wants to kiss me and I want him to. Yet for a long time
we hold hands and stare at each other. The moon drifts
across the sky—not in the same place when Hayden first
came to talk with me on the balcony. I'm aware that music
floats around us, and I'm not sure if it's the Ancestors
singing or the speakers drumming a rhythm. Hayden
moves closer, and after what seems like the longest wait
of my life, his lips gently touch mine, and I know I will
never leave his side.

CHAPTER THREE

Tamarind Stew

My mother sucks her teeth and walks past Hayden when she sees him sitting on the balcony with me. He looks at me, puzzled, as she hurriedly strides past him, ignoring him like he's an irrelevant stone on the road. I turn and glance uncomfortably at him, trying to think of something to say. Words are stuck in my mouth; I don't know how to tell him she is like this with all men. Before I can explain, Vee quietly saunters into the yard. While my mother is the epitome of femininity, Vee's masculine stance leaves no doubt about her sexuality. Hayden's mouth opens wide in shock. His eyes grow large as he takes in everything.

He turns to me. There is a look of absolute disbelief
on his face. Under his gaze, I twitch uncomfortably; this
is the moment I've feared—the one I've been dreading
since we met. I now have to explain their relationship. I
don't know how to tell him about them, and I find myself
stuttering the first word, unable to make a
coherent sentence.

Vee sees that I'm stumbling. She stops for a moment
and takes in our clasped hands and the way our bodies
quietly touch. Despite the uncomfortable circumstance,
she notices that my eyes are shining because of this boy
sitting next to me. Unlike my mother, she doesn't ignore
Hayden, but instead stops and talks to us.

"Hi, Kai." Her voice is calm, like this is an everyday
occurrence. "I see you have a new friend. Who is he?"

I shift in my seat. "Vee, this is my boyfriend, Hayden."

"I guess he's the reason for your Mammie's loud
chupps?" she asks. I nod.

"Well, you would think she'd be ready for this with you
so shockingly pretty!"

She looks him up and down. "Hi, Hayden. I'm Vee. It's
nice to meet you."

Hayden stares at Vee. Her eyes rest on his green eyes
and she turns to me. "Kai, you have a pretty boy. Men like
him will break plenty of hearts."

"Vee, please . . ."

"Let me say what I have to say," Vee interrupts. "Kai
hasn't told us anything about you, and it's like she's

keeping you to herself. Why is that? How y'all meet?
When did this all begin?"

I answer for Hayden. "I met him at Brittany's house.
He's her cousin."

Vee raises her eyebrows and looks him directly in the
eye. "What's your last name?"

When Hayden tells her, she shakes her head. "I don't
know what to say because I truly wonder if anything good
can come of this."

Hayden and I squirm.

"Do your parents know that Kai is your girlfriend?"

Under her scrutiny Hayden is uncomfortable. I answer
for him, "Vee, please don't ask these questions."

"What is this!" she exclaims. "That answers everything!
I don't need to ask what they've said, but I can guess.
Everybody on this little island knows his snobbish family
doesn't allow any and everybody to enter through their
front door. I can bet on my last dollar that you can't take
Kai home. I know that Hayden's mother doesn't sleep
when night comes 'cause she's worrying and worrying that
her handsome green-eyed son spends his time with some
dark-skin girl who lives in places she never visits."

She shakes her head, studying our downfallen faces.
"Cheer up, pickney. Things not all that bad. What a
generation y'all are! You don't think about what you do.
You don't care for tradition—y'all just a live life."

Hayden is silent. I don't say anything. This isn't the
first time we've heard this. Since that night on Brittany's
balcony when we proclaimed our love for each other, life

became very different. Hayden frequently hears about his mother's concern that he is seeing a girl whose mother was once a maid. At school, there is total shock and disbelief that the scholarship girl snagged the trophy green-eyed boy, who is every girl's dream.

Vee calls to my mother, but there is no answer.

"Excuse me. I'm going to get Kai's Mammie 'cause she need to meet you. My woman is stubborn like a mule. Hold on, I'll be right back."

Hayden eyes me; he wants an explanation, but before I can speak, Vee drags my mother outside to meet him. My mother stares angrily at Hayden. I feel awkward introducing her. There is suspicion written all over her eyes. Although he is uncomfortable under her glare, he can't control his curiosity, and he stares at her and Vee.

Vee tells her his last name. My mother raises surprised eyebrows, then notices that he is transfixed by her and Vee.

"Kai never tell you that she live in a house that have only woman," my mother barks. Hayden doesn't answer. She forgets her reverence for him and his family name because she doesn't like his hand around my waist.

"This here is my house"—her voice is much louder—"and me don't apologize one bit for how me live. If you think we not right or something like that, it's best you leave."

"You don't see me going anywhere, do you?" Hayden's tone is calm.

"Good, this settled." My mother goes into the house.

Vee watches her then looks at us. "Okay, things seem fine for now. I'm going to leave you two alone."

There is a long silence after they leave.

"Wow!" he finally says.

"Is that wow good or wow bad?"

"Neither. It's just wow! When someone has parents, you have this image of what they're like. I just never ever imagined that it'd be anyone like them. Why didn't you say something?"

"What could I say? How do I explain it?"

"I understand. Believe me, I do. Women don't live together on this island, because it just doesn't happen. Women love men and that's the way it goes. As far as most people are concerned, things like this only happen in big countries, and that's why I didn't expect it. But you could have warned me. Believe me, I wouldn't have run away from you if I learned about it, but at least I'd be prepared for them."

"Hayden, it's just not easy to explain this, them, us. For most of my life, I've been ostracized because of them. People are very judgmental." I turn to him. My voice is hushed as I ask, "Does it matter to you?"

I'm so afraid of his response.

"No, it doesn't." His words are sure and unwavering.

"It wasn't easy for me," I confide. "People still stare and point at my mother like she's a freak. And they think I'm weird too."

"Kai, people are always talking on this island. It's their favourite pastime—*he say this, she say that*. I know you're not a freak, and they will soon learn that your mother must have done something right because you have the hottest man on the island for your boyfriend." Then he throws his arm around my shoulder and we both laugh.

As he bends over to kiss me, I hear some shuffling, and through the corner of my eyes, I see my mother peeking at us from behind the curtains. Vee tries to pull her away from the window, but my mother pushes her aside.

That night, through the thin wall that divides our rooms, my mother tosses and turns in her bed.

I hear her whispering to Vee, "Me can't believe that she bring that red boy to this house. And where he get that posh-sounding name? Me don't know no one who name them pickney Hayden."

"It shocked me too! People like that red boy don't want to be seen with people like us."

"Nothing good will come from this, and me worried for Kai."

"Don't say that. The world is changing. He looks like he really likes Kai."

"But men never mean well."

Vee tries to calm her. But nothing she says offers comfort. My mother sounds more and more agitated.

Then the door to their room opens, my doorknob turns, and my mother is in my room. Her forehead is creased like the worn hide of an old cow. I sit up on the bed, and she joins me.

She lies down next to me, like when I was a child who

was frightened of the night. I feel her worry on the cracks on her forehead. As I touch each crevice, her thoughts seep into my mind, so I'm not surprised when she finally speaks.

"Kai, I knew one day you'd bring some man home. That is the natural course of things, and with you so pretty and all, me just hope after hope that he is one good man. But I never expected it to be a red boy from that society family. I used to work for his kinda people. I used to clean their houses and know things that you don't understand. I hear how them think. Man who come from places like that red boy use girls like you. He can't bring you home."

"Mammie, I love Hayden. He loves me. Why is it, though I am in love for the first time in my life, the world has become harsh?"

"Kai, what you know about love at this point in life? Nothing, my child. All you know is that the blood a-rush through you veins fast fast. I'm warning you, Kai, love not easy."

"You don't understand. Hayden is so different to anyone I've known."

"Kai, this is what I have to say. Not too many good man in this world. Maybe he one of them, but don't count on that. I've been telling you that since you born 'cause I don't want you to live your life in disappointment. Go to school. Do well there and then think about a boyfriend. If you follow me, then you go have a good life."

"Hayden is different."

Her eyes are in some far-off world. "Kai, love sweet. I know that for sure. It real sweet but it make woman turn fooly and stupid. I see it time after time. The first time you love, you believe that it too good to be true, but this is the truth that none of them tell you, love takes work, and lots and lots of work. Do you know why nobody talk about Adam and Eve after them did join? 'Cause people know they did fight. For all we know, they gone them separate way after they make some pickney. I'm not stupid like so many woman. I learned quick. Never trust no man, them all bad."

My mother sent me to school to learn. My mind absorbed language and I also became adept at math and can easily add sums. Ever since I was a child, I learned that in my mother's world there are many walls, and she believes not all need to be scaled. She always says that men are the cause of all problems. If her life was an equation, and you put all the pieces together, her statement is true. Her equation is comprised of three expressions: in the first set, her father never remembered that he had a daughter; in the second, her mother never sent her to school, as she needed her help to look after her brothers; and in the final expression, her lover deserted her and their child. Add these together, and you get a very bad outcome. By the time I met Hayden, the occasional man who climbed the steps to our house was a family member. Even our female dog growls if a man comes to the gate.

On this little island of colossal beauty with a history of conquest and slavery, happy endings are hard to find. I know this to be true because the Ancestors seldom tell me stories that make me smile; sadly, the past is filled with tragedy. We have become like pollen blowing in the wind; a people who drift freely and fall on an object, hoping the flower will fertilize. The Ancestors whisper that people on this island hold the past and all its injustices as an excuse. They know this because they once lived here; they caused pain; some drank till they fell on the ground, and many had children they forgot. They've whispered that it's time for us to realize that this equation, the one that began when we came across the Atlantic on a slave ship, needs to have a new expression to cancel out the past. As much as they know this to be true, they notice that no schoolroom has rewritten this archaic equation.

It saddens them that there is a legacy where boys do not learn how to become men, and girls are taught to stand alone. Men and women congregate at separate sides of the equal sign, with expressions that don't balance. And they do not realize that sometimes you need to tweak the equation and play with the numbers to make it balance.

The Ancestors tell me that a man chooses not to become a man. He decides to ignore the equation and pretend that it cannot be solved. And when he openly adopts this belief, the easiest place to bite is a woman's breast.

This is the world of my mother. This is the world of woman. This is the equation that they can't solve, no matter how much they try to and it wears on their faces and bodies. At a very young age, I was very aware something was amiss. Although the Ancestors talk to me and teach me so much about life, I don't need them to explain this pain. I am a product of it.

I cannot help but think about the life I'm given. My father is not around; he left long ago, before I could even say, "Daddy." I don't know what his face looks like or the sound of his voice. One day I may walk past him on Market Street—casually gaze upon the man who is my father and not even know.

I've spent hours working on my equation, wanting desperately to make it balance by reviewing the numbers. In speaking with the Ancestors, I made a determination that my equation is solvable, and when I reworked it, his absence was no longer a deep ache.

My mother is still a young woman when I meet Hayden, and when she sees him, she instantly loathes him because he is a man; he is the side of her equation that doesn't work. She can't conceive there is any good in him. She keeps reminding me that stories are not always happy. But I am a storyteller who believes that stories have no endings, and for the first time in my life her words clash with mine.

When Hayden enters through the front door, the look of shock on his face makes me hang my head in shame. My handsome boyfriend only knows the world of grand houses—large, airy rooms and servants. He's never considered the lives of the maids who cook or clean. At this moment, I feel the gap that separates us; the one that everyone keeps reminding us exists. The truth is so blatant, since my whole street can fit into Hayden's yard and there would still be ample room left over to build a large house with a beautiful garden.

"I shouldn't have invited you," I say.

"No, no, Kai. I'm glad you did." His words are slow. He surveys the bare, unfinished wooden walls that never touch the roof, his eyes uneasily shifting around the house. For the first time in his life, he is a Christmas ornament displayed at Easter.

"Our worlds are different, and it's more than just my mother and Vee," I say to break the silence. "You grew up with a maid to make dumplings, while I was taught how to cook them. Your hands never washed clothes, while mine know how bleach can toughen the skin. You bought imported apples and grapes at the supermarket, while I climbed a tree for mangoes."

"Yes, we are different," he mutters slowly. Then he looks at me, his face intense. "But does it matter?"

I don't reply. I want him to answer his question. He sees me looking at him, waiting, but I don't respond. And after a few minutes, he finally speaks.

"Kai, I don't give a damn that you live in a part of the island that I didn't know existed, or that you can climb a tree better than me. So what if your mother doesn't like men? Yes, everything about you and your life is new to me, but who cares? None of that matters. And it really doesn't, because we have each other."

In that moment we both realize that for our equation to work, we have to reassess myths to allow our love to survive. Hayden learns that the roads he was taught to avoid, led to me, and through Hayden a door opens that broadens the world I know. As our feet walk into a space that has no walls, ceilings or floors, we determine the equation, reworking the numbers to find the balance. At this time in our lives, we have not yet entered adulthood; our bodies and minds are still forming. While in school, I had a teacher who once said that equations have finite possibilities; through Hayden, I begin to realize that isn't really true.

It is a hot afternoon when Hayden and I first make tamarind stew. The sun is directly above when he arrives with a bag of tamarinds in his hand. Before we met, I'd pick tamarinds off the tree and eat them. Tamarinds have an overpowering sourness that is peppered by a faint sweetness, and I enjoy bombarding my senses with their distinctive taste. Hayden loves tamarind stew because he can disguise the bitterness with brown sugar.

Hayden is in a mischievous mood as we shell the fruit. He keeps tickling and touching me, while I try to be serious about the task at hand. As we finish shelling the tamarinds and put them in the pot to boil, his hands linger on my abdomen and we look at each other in a way that makes me aware of our desire. It's a silent moment in which I'm conscious of my body and his body, and the feelings that he's opened up in me.

As the pot simmers on the stove, he pulls my hand and leads me away. As our bodies move, the tamarinds melt in the water. They merge and bubble till the cover of the pot clinks from the steam. The stew thickens; it simmers in the pot; heat grows and grows until it explodes; the pot is on fire. We smell it and run into the kitchen, nude and sweaty, our laughter echoing inside the walls of my small house as we douse the flames.

The burnt pot does not stop our desire, and a few days later we attempt to make tamarind stew again. While the pot simmers, I sit on the kitchen counter. Hayden stands in front of me. With my arms wrapped around his shoulders, we both peer into the pot and see the tamarinds dissolve and thicken. After he pours brown sugar into the stew, his lips taste of steam. When it cools, Hayden dips his hand into the pot. I lick the stew from his fingers. While we eat, a soft breeze blows and caresses our skin.

When my period doesn't come, Hayden shrugs and says it's late. I'm not sure. I walk around the house in a stupor. Each morning when I awake, I run to the bathroom, hoping to see a sign of blood. But there is none. Soon different scents begin to make me nauseous. I am afraid to go to Hayden. My mother notices my withdrawal and moodiness and realizes my condition. She sits me down and shakes her head. I stare at the floor. I don't want to see her expression.

"Are you and Hayden playing in big-people business, eh Kai?" she asks.

I nod my head, afraid to speak.

"There are things you take so these things don't happen."

Then I start to cry.

"Calm down child. Calm down. We'll figure this out. I've heard about some tea that might work. We'll try it and see what happens."

Later that day, she brings me something hot to drink. Her eyes are worried, and she looks at me with earnest.

"Kai, don't get me wrong 'cause I don't want to encourage you in this, but I was no older than you when I gave birth. This is what I know: you're still a child and don't need one. You have to finish school. Do as I say right now—you have to trust me on this."

I feel as if I want to spit out the bitter tea, but I swallow each drop. My mother watches me with concern. Soon my insides begin to hurt and my womb contracts; she lies next to me. She stays with me, and after the sun rises, my blood flows.

I don't tell Hayden about the tea. As much as I love him, I'm unsure of his reaction, but he knows something is amiss. He sees me withdraw and also knows my blood is flowing again. He comes to my house, and we just sit and don't talk; our conversation is lost. I don't even want him to touch me or come close. A silence invades our relationship, and when we're together, I never look at him as I stare into the sky, unable to notice its vast blueness, ashamed of everything that has happened.

"What are you thinking? What's going on in your pretty little head?" Hayden pursues.

"Why do you want to know?"

"Kai, we need to talk about what happened."

"What are you talking about?"

"Don't pretend that it didn't happen. I know it did."

We are both silent after he speaks. I say nothing for a while. I realize that Hayden knows. But I can't turn my head and look at him.

"One day, you and I will have pretty children," he finally says, breaking our silence. "I think about it. I honestly do."

"I didn't know you knew."

"Of course, I did. I saw all the signs, and like you I didn't know how to deal with it. It's too much for us now. We got so caught up in everything that we didn't take any precautions."

"I have moments when I question everything."

"Kai, so do I, but we'll be careful so that this doesn't happen again. You taught me that you write your own endings. Let's make sure we create ours."

He pulls me to him, and this time I don't push him away. I look up at the sky. The clouds are still there— small puffy ones that float easily and innocently. I feel the strength of Hayden's strong body, and I move closer into

his warm safety. As I look up again, I realize there are
always clouds but behind them is an immense blue sky.

Hayden spends the day with me. We're being foolish
and exceptionally playful. He takes a jug of red juice and
pretends to drink it with the cap on. As he turns the
bottle upside down, the cap is loose and falls off. The red
drink spills all over the clothes he intends to wear to a
party that night. I laugh at his predicament. We clean
up the mess in a jovial mood and continue this gaiety
as he drives up the hill to his house to change clothes.
Lights shimmer in the background as his car climbs the
hill that distances us from the city. Hayden's house comes
into view. Built when sugar was king of the island, this
colonial architecture has a majestic appearance with its
large windows and porch.

He parks in the driveway. I look at him. "I'll wait here
for you."

Although Hayden and I are always together, if there
is ever an occasion when he needs to get something from
home while I'm with him, I wait in the car.

"No, you won't," he insists. "Maybe it's time you
see inside."

"How do you think they'll react?"

Hayden pulls my arm. "I don't care. They probably
aren't even home. My father's never around, so the only
person who'll be there is my mother. And it's about time
she meets you."

I shake my head to protest, but Hayden grabs me and pulls me with him. As I put my trembling hand in his, he squeezes it, reassuring me that everything will be fine. Silently I'm thinking that although both of our ancestors once worked on this estate, his left the hard work in the field while mine continued to labour on the land.

"It's magnificent!" I exclaim from the balcony, gazing at the view. In front of me, the lights of St. John's appear like a giant Christmas tree as they sparkle in the distance. Beyond that lies the darkness of the sea, and with the moon high in the sky, its beams hit the water, making it magically glisten.

He smiles. "I grew up with it and I guess I've forgotten how pretty it is." He stands looking at it for a moment and reflects, "We'll sit here once I've finished dressing. It's been awhile since I've done that."

The house is from a bygone era, with its large stone walls and strong columns. Flowers fill the entrance, and an archway leads into the living room. Following Hayden, we enter a tasteful, elegant room that is like a picture in a foreign magazine. The cushions on the chairs are fluffy and inviting. Beautiful paintings of island scenes adorn all the walls. The room breathes the long history and wealth of the family, and it silently whispers of exclusion.

Suddenly Hayden and I hear a sound. Realizing we are not alone, we turn in shock. To our surprise, in one corner of the room his mother is sitting in a chair, while his father, a man whose presence overpowers the room, is standing in another area. No one speaks. Everyone is looking at me. I feel like a nude painting on the wall.

I look for the door and feel this desperate desire to flee, run from this room, from this house, from these people. They stare at me, not making any initiative to introduce themselves or say, "Hi." Hayden stands motionless. I know he feels trapped. His hands clamp around mine. Then as if some strange spirit takes hold of him, he grabs my hand and walks me over to his father.

As I get closer to him, I feel as if I'm seeing a twin image, they look so much alike. Hayden carries not just his father's eyes and face; their body structure and height are the same; they also hold their heads in the same regal style.

"This is Kai, my girlfriend," Hayden says.

This man looks at me. Though his eyes mimic Hayden's, I cannot read or understand his expression. I extend my hand. He looks scornfully at it. Awaiting his acknowledgment, my hand feels heavy in mid-air. He turns his head away. Then his mother snickers. Hayden looks at her, then at his father. He takes my hand that sits frozen in the air and wraps it in his. He looks his father in the eye as he takes my palm, lifts it to his lips and kisses each finger.

He yells at him, "This is Kai. I love her. Don't you want to meet the woman your son spends his time with?"

"Why?" his father retorts. "There will be other women, so we don't need to know anyone right now. She is just a passing phase."

I can feel Hayden's anger as he pulls me out of the room and walks quickly along the corridors of this grand house. I don't recall much else. I know we go to his room, where he changes his clothes. He does not speak, and his mood shifts. I cannot read his mind. For the first time, I am face-to-face with Hayden's world, and we are, again, realizing this equation needs balancing.

By the time this incident occurs, our relationship is mature, we've been boyfriend and girlfriend for two years. I understand Hayden and his motivations. I know the thoughts that are shifting through this mind as he tries to make sense of his parents' action. He is not embarrassed by them; he's often shared with me their hostility towards our relationship. But right now I feel the anger emanating from him.

After he changes his clothes, we hurriedly leave. Quickly walking past the beautiful view, we forget to sit and enjoy it—desperate to say goodbye to this place. Our jovial mood dissipated, we drive to the party in silence. Hayden is wrapped in his thoughts. I am wrapped in mine. Our thoughts are the same, even though we don't voice them.

We arrive at the party, but a knife has sliced us. Hayden goes to the bar. With a sense of unease, I watch him from a distance. There is chatter around us, pretty clips of conversation that I don't want to hear. I need to escape into my thoughts. I find a dark corner where I can be alone. Brittany is at the party and sees Hayden and I are apart. She comes to me.

"Kai, are you okay? Did you and Hayden have a fight?"
I shake my head. I still can't speak.

"What happened?" she asks. I can hear the concern in her voice.

"Hayden took me to his home, and . . . his parents were there, and they weren't very nice to us—"

I can't finish the words.

Her caring arms quickly pull me to her—her body warm and reassuring. "I know, Kai. Don't say anymore. I can guess how they treated you. You don't have to tell me. They've been very upset about you and Hayden."

"But *why*? *Why* are they like this?"

"They just care about what people think. It's so damn stupid. Why can't we be free to love who we love? My parents did what they wanted and look how happy they are."

As we talk, Hayden's best friend, Shaun, joins us.

He says, "They say it's Obeah that has Hayden so crazy about you, but I'm not so sure. You look so damn enticing in this dress. You just so sweet to look at. I hope you girls don't mind me joining you, but I couldn't resist. You are the two prettiest faces in the room."

Brittany and I don't respond, because we don't want him around. He knows he is interrupting us but doesn't care. Shaun is very flirtatious. His eyes are in constant motion appraising women. He's been known to be with several at one time. He never hides that he finds me very appealing, often voicing this to Hayden. It doesn't bother Hayden. Shaun behaves like that around all women.

Every time we meet him, he has a new woman on his arm, but they never last long. There was a time when Brittany had a crush on him. I'm truly thankful that nothing evolved from it. I'm aware that she still likes him, and I pray that ember will never find a light.

I look around the room and see Hayden. He looks over and sees Shaun by my side. His face becomes anxious; he rushes to me and pushes his friend away. We stand face-to-face; words hang in the air. So much needs to be said, but we don't know how. He holds me with urgency. I feel the strength of his chest, the warmth of his body. I don't want to leave the comfort of his embrace. Shaun looks at us and laughs. He thinks his friend's love for me is too consuming. Brittany sighs with relief when she sees we're together.

This closeness from being engulfed in Hayden's powerful arms reminds me that once no outside forces are attacking us, we are fine. And I want to believe we will always be fine.

Later that night, alone at home, I dip my ears into the wind and wait for the sound of the Ancestors. They quickly come to me, but on that night, I don't want to hear their voices. This time I tell them my thoughts.

I've lived two lives: one before I met Hayden and another after. I love that he always listens to my stories and everything I say; he is the keeper of my deepest confidences. He is one of the few people who knows I began writing stories at eight or that when I learned to read, I found the pictures in the book more exciting than the words because the plots all sounded the same: there was always a princess being saved by a prince. Hayden is the first man I kissed. His eyes are alert, captivating everyone around him, but they shine when he is with me. We are so intertwined that it appears we can't do without each other. Many mornings, before the sun rises, he drives from his grandiose house at the top of a hill to my small dwelling to lightly throw pebbles at my bedroom window. When the delicate tapping wakes me, I peek through the drapes to see him standing next to his car—an impatient look on his face. Sneaking past my mother's room, fearful of waking her and Vee, I quietly tiptoe to the front door to be with him. Once he sees me, Hayden gently touches my lips; he tastes of the early-morning dew. Our hands are clasped as we drive to the beach. His golden shade contrasts with my dark, ebony complexion.

At the seashore, we spread a blanket on the powdery, white sand and wait for sunrise. These mornings transport us from our home, an island ten miles wide and ten miles long with a ragged coastline that creates hundreds of small, intimate coves with pristine beaches where the sound of the waves breaking on the shore mesmerizes us with its sweet tranquillity. With Hayden's body pressed into mine, we sit at the seashore—the endless horizon stretching in front of us—forgetting that he is a "light-skinned" boy who comes from a "good family," while I am the illegitimate child of a "dark-skinned" woman who never finished school. Though this should be incidental and trivial, it isn't. Our home is not a place that forgets history. Here it thrives and seeps into the pores of its inhabitants, creating walls so high that people often wonder if they can ever be scaled.

This is the tale that I tell the Ancestors. And they listen. That night, they don't tell me any stories as my life merges into their infinite world of stories.

CHAPTER FOUR

Hayden's Hill

In his house at the top of a hill, the view was so spectacular that as early as six years old Hayden believed he lived in paradise. He could see the island's rolling hills merge into one another. The green shrubs ran into more foliage, to create an unending sea of green occasionally dotted with red-and-silver rooftops, and his young eyes told him that the sky lightly touched the water at the horizon, fusing into a sheet of blue. Each day, as it danced along the galvanized roofs, the glory of the rising sun sent shimmering rays into town.

As a boy, he played on the veranda, with his mother watching over him. She blissfully smiled at his childish fascination with the view and gently placed him in her lap, where they looked at the surrounding countryside. At night, snuggling into her warmth, he'd sit on the balcony, lifting his head to see a dazzling spectrum above.

"Look," he said to his mother, "there's a city in the sky." His mother patiently replied, "No, Hayden. There isn't another world up there. Those are stars twinkling in the night."

But his childish mind didn't believe her, because he liked to think that there was a metropolis in the heavens.

Whether it was night or day, Hayden's mother always pointed out the landmark Anglican cathedral. Poised on a small incline, this church, with the architectural magnificence of its two distinct steeples, dominated the landscape. This imposing building, built over a hundred years ago, replaced the previous place of worship, which was destroyed by an earthquake over a century ago. The new cathedral was designed to be earthquake proof, and it waited over a hundred years to prove its sturdiness.

Hayden's family had a long history in this church. He was christened there. His parents stood at its altar and swore eternal love. His grandparents, great-grandparents and great-great grandparents also shared that fate.

When slavery ruled the land, the plantation owners commanded the slaves to convert to Christianity, fearing the African religion, where the spells and entrenched spiritual practices of Obeah's men seemed more powerful than the Christian faith. The landowners had heard about, and some witnessed, supernatural forces that made dead men walk and stones rise from their resting place on the ground to hit objects. Even today, Obeah is quietly practised, but the remnants of this landowning class and the former slaves worshipped at the same church, but never at the same hour.

The early Sunday-morning service was frequented by the people whose skin was a pale contrast to those who attended the later mass. Hayden's family were early-morning folk, and this was not just because their skin had lost most of its darker hue through interracial marriages. The distinct difference between Hayden's family and the majority of the population was their immense wealth.

Hayden's great-great-great grandfather, Thomas I, was an aristocratic English gentleman, whose family held several business interests in England; he hadn't needed to go afar to seek his fortune. However, a restlessness inside of him made him acutely aware he didn't want the pastoral life associated with nobility. At a very young age, he decided to carve out a distinct niche for himself, far from the confines of his family name, and this led him to the British colonies. Antigua was his first port of call, and when he arrived, he contacted a family friend, who immediately issued a dinner invitation. Thomas eagerly accepted it, anticipating fresh food like roasted chicken and vegetables after the bland sailing diet of salted pork and crackers. As he prepared to go to his friend's house, he was unaware that this meeting would dramatically change the course of his life.

That night, Hayden's great-great-great grandfather cast his eyes on Margaret, the exceptionally beautiful, illegitimate daughter that his family friend had with a mulatto slave. He was immediately taken with the hue of her golden-brown skin and her long-cascading hair, which fell into soft ringlets around her face. Her mesmerizing aqua eyes shocked him, holding him captive. Never having seen anyone more lovely, he couldn't help but stare unabashedly. When she smiled at him, his heart beat so fast he felt his mouth go dry. The girl's father eagerly took in the young man's lustiness, Margaret's positive response to this man's attention, and his own burning desire to see his beloved daughter married into acceptable society.

Later that evening, as the two men enjoyed an after-dinner drink, the host put his plan into action.

"Thomas," he said, "I insist that you stay. I understand you've travelled to seek your fortune in the colonies. I must confess that I admire your independent nature, for I'm well aware, considering your family's great wealth, that you don't need to be living in this dreadful heat. I have a thriving business here, and I'm in desperate need of assistance. If you stay and help me, I'll make it worth your while with a handsome salary. We don't need to speak about this to anyone. It will be between us. This will allow you to get a better understanding about how business is run in the colonies and also prepare you for starting your own. There's plenty of room in the house. It'll be a true delight to have you stay while you settle in."

"Edward, this is a very kind and generous offer. I'm speechless and don't know what to say. I truly don't wish to impose."

"If I didn't want you here, I wouldn't have asked you. Let's not discuss this any further. You're staying, and that's settled."

On a tiny island, a world so different from the one he'd known—a place where cane fields looked like a magical carpet when it blows in the hot, lush breeze—Thomas, for the first time in his life, didn't feel like he was rebelling; he was comfortable with the soft breeze cooling his skin and the way the land sloped on the hill. He liked the feel of his sweat as it poured down his face. It was as if his foot had found the right shoe. He took to running the business with such natural ease that Edward grew more impressed and knew his plan could easily work.

As the weeks passed, Thomas's passion for Margaret didn't diminish; in fact, it grew into a raging obsession. Hayden's great-great-great grandfather was a young man with very lustful thoughts, and this aqua-eyed woman with golden skin so captured his imagination her image was with him from dawn to dusk. Whenever he saw Margaret, his thoughts were totally impure, as he pictured her golden thighs wrapped around his paler complexion. Her mesmerizing eyes wove a spell, and every morning he looked forward to waking, because he knew he'd soon gaze into the eyes of her loveliness. At night, he fell asleep believing that there would come a time when he'd lie down and stare into her beautiful face. Each day their shy smiles grew into lingering looks.

Early one morning, Thomas's passion drove him to do the unthinkable, abandoning all reason, sneaking into Margaret's room. When she heard the door, her head turned in surprise. Margaret said nothing as her eyes locked with his light-blue ones. As she'd just finished her bath, small droplets of water clung to her golden skin, enhancing the sinuous curves of her body. She quietly dropped the towel, and Thomas just stared at her, unsure what to do. He was steps away from touching her smooth, rounded breasts. His eyes devoured her, and as he was about to touch her, he heard Edward call his name. They looked at each other in desperation. Shaking his head, Thomas slipped out of the room.

Thomas was now truly possessed. Margaret's golden image flashed through his mind every thirty seconds. He couldn't focus or think. All he wanted to do was lie on a bed with her. Thomas was so obsessed that he was forgetting the scandal he'd cause if he married an illegitimate, mixed woman.

On that same evening, with her golden skin dancing in his eyes and his lust out of control, Thomas finally spoke with his host.

"Edward, your daughter is the most beautiful woman I've ever laid my eyes on," he gushed. "Forgive me for saying this, and I mean no disrespect, but I think of Margaret all the time."

"Thomas, I confess that I worry about her future. As

you know, I'm a married man, and I assure you this child is the fruit of my loins, although she is the child of a slave. My wife left for London years ago because she couldn't bear to look at my daughter. You see, my wife is barren and this hurt her so much. It saddens me that we only see each other when I'm in London. Yet my daughter's sweet spirit and unsurpassed beauty brings me great joy, and I love her dearly. As she is my only child, my wish is to see her settled before I die.

"I haven't said anything yet to you, but I desire to live my last days in London with my wife. However, I cannot leave until I've married Margaret to a worthy man. When she was born and I saw her eyes, I took her from her mother and brought her to this house to be raised as my child. I've seen to her education. She is a literate woman. But alas, I fear men will turn away because her blood is not pure."

"Edward, she is the most beautiful woman I've seen. Though I have a great family name, I have nothing to offer such an exquisite woman."

"Thomas, I am an old man and I want to die peacefully. One is never sure how much time he has on this earth, and I only ask the good Lord to allow me to get back to my wife's side in London. That is why I'm offering you a large dowry. Marry Margaret and I will turn over the deed to this house, the general store and all of the land I own on the island to you. I don't need these anymore, as I already have wealth in London to last my lifetime. You're familiar with my operations and know that these are all profitable ventures. This is not a vast fortune, but it is a good life. With time it will build you wealth like it did for me. I know it's a small token for a man of your breeding, but you've found love, and believe me, this is a reward you can never replace."

Two days later Thomas, a young man with a long-standing aristocratic background, married the beautiful, illegitimate mixed daughter of a wealthy landowner and inherited a small fortune on a tiny Caribbean island. In his obsession, he forgot to think of how this act would impact his family. When news of this marriage reached his mother in her grand country manor in England, she fainted. Then she took a pen and wrote him a letter that made its way across the Atlantic Ocean to Thomas.

When he received it, Thomas immediately recognized his mother's neat handwriting and quickly opened the letter. His mother wished him well in his marriage but was aghast to learn that he'd married an illegitimate woman with Negro blood. His action was a scandal. He'd smeared the family's good name, and she never wished to hear from him again. She was sending him a large sum of money to settle his inheritance. He was never to return to London or contact his family, because through this marriage he was now dead to them.

After he read and reread the letter, Thomas looked out at the spectacular view from his balcony and then at his even more beautiful wife. He had known his mother would be upset but couldn't understand how she'd renounce her own child.

Although he experienced lust and joy with Margaret, he'd never spoken about the importance of his family name. With the letter in his hand, he decided that she'd never need to learn about his background and he tore the letter into small shreds, tossed it into the wind and watched the cool Antiguan breeze take away each little scrap of paper. A few months later when he received his inheritance, he deposited a large sum of money at the bank. The manager assumed this considerable deposit was part of the large dowry that was needed for a gentleman like Thomas to marry a woman with Negro blood. Knowing what was going on in this man's head, Thomas said nothing. That night he smiled in contentment in the afterglow of the very steamy lovemaking with his beautiful wife; England was far away; the tropics was his life and he felt truly blessed with his new identity.

His happiness was short-lived. While giving birth to their second child, Margaret died, then the baby died. Thomas cried in total despair when their coffins were lowered into the ground. It was the small hand of his only child, Thomas II, that kept him from jumping into her grave. Thomas Sr. worked hard, and his holdings grew exponentially. When he proudly escorted his son to university in London, he returned as a very wealthy man. Even if he hadn't been born into his social circle and carried the manners of an aristocrat, he'd be accepted because of his vast holdings. More than twenty years had

passed, and his mother was no longer alive. Thomas had
a longing to reconnect with his family and felt that surely
his action was long forgotten. He felt a strong desire to
speak with his brother and tell him about his life during
the years of their separation, because they were once
very close. He also wanted his only son to know that he
had family. For all those reasons, Thomas Sr. returned to
England, making an unannounced visit to his brother
at the very grand house where he was born. His son, a
slightly darker version of himself, stood next to him when
he knocked at his family estate. Since his father rarely
spoke of his birthplace, this was the first time this child
learned of his father's background. That's why Thomas Jr.
was shocked by the size and magnificence of his father's
family estate. When the door finally opened, recognizing
the family resemblance, the maid invited them in.

It was with great pride that Thomas Sr. introduced
his son and boasted of his scholastic achievements. This
man looked at his brother, then at his golden-coloured
nephew, and firmly reminded them that they were no
longer family, for he could never accept a child of mixed
blood as part of their aristocratic bloodline. Thomas heard
his brother's words, and when he looked at his eyes, he
saw an anger he didn't understand. He didn't say anything
as he left his family estate. Neither father nor son looked
back as they walked away from the magnificent home of
Thomas's birthright. When he could no longer see his
grand family home, Thomas finally found his voice and
told his only son to forget his father's heritage.

When his grandson, Thomas III, was born, Thomas I
saw he'd inherited his grandmother's aqua eyes, and he
cried because he realized how much he still missed her.
Margaret's eyes were the last image he remembered when
he died.

With its large windows, airy rooms and spacious
veranda, Hayden's home boasts the best view on the island
and an interesting history that the occupants of this grand
home and the people of the island never forgot. Everyone
was aware of Hayden's family's important status. Hayden's
family has many traditions—one being that the firstborn
male must be named Thomas. This tradition lasted for
four generations, until the birth of Hayden.

The large Anglican cathedral was one of the
centrepieces of Hayden's young life. His father seldom
attended service, but his mother was a stringently
religious woman, who felt that knowledge of God was
an essential foundation. Hayden was christened in that
imposing cathedral and, from that moment, had no choice
regarding his religious upbringing. Early every Sunday
morning, his mother woke him to attend church. After
he'd grown tired of listening to the priest's monotonous
babble about the soul or watching the women in large-
brimmed hats fan themselves, his young frame often fell
asleep in the pews. His mother always nudged him, giving
him a stern, reproachful look when his body relaxed into
the hard pew.

He knew the faces of the regular churchgoers and watched as they sat prissily in their seats in their well-pressed frocks with folds and seams stiff from starch. Their well-coiffed hair was the work of the hot iron and curlers that urged their locks to fall into a nicely manicured style that was perfectly prim and proper for mass. Entranced by the words of the priest, these women sat immobile, like mannequins, but fifteen minutes into the sermon their stillness was defeated by a trickle of sweat that quietly slid down the side of their face.

Hayden was taught to pray for thankfulness before meals. Each night at his bedtime, his mother knelt with him to ask for his soul's guidance. She extended the traditional prayer as she pleaded with the Lord to keep her son pious so that he remained on the path of righteousness. Hayden's knees often ached after kneeling for extended periods of time, but he learned it was best not to complain, because if he did, his mother made him continue to pray so that he'd repent for thinking impure thoughts. Whenever he committed a venial sin or acted in a selfish manner, his mother made him bend in supplication to correct his wrongdoings.

Despite the gruelling church service and lengthy prayers, Hayden loved Sundays. Only at that time was his whole family together. They all sat in the grand dining room over a scrumptious lunch of his favourite foods, like macaroni and cheese, and a dessert of coconut cake. His father always sat at the head of the table and bent his

head when his mother said grace. As they ate, his father
talked about the shops he owned and occasionally asked
his son and daughter about their week. His mother, at the
opposite end of the table, quietly ate and never said
a word.

After lunch, the family retreated to the large porch and
the house came to life with visitors. On Sunday afternoons, a steady stream of family and friends always drove
up the steep incline, to visit this beautiful-looking family
and the beautiful view.

Before the visitors came, young Hayden often asked
his father to play with him, but his father just patted him
on his head and said, "Later." Always preoccupied with
outside affairs, Thomas V forgot to spend time kicking
the ball with Hayden or showing him how to use a bat.
Instead, he bought his only son toys, but Hayden longed
for his father's attention. As a child, he looked to this
man with wide-eyed adoration. Whenever his father
promised he'd be home early to kick the ball with him,
he'd sit patiently on the veranda, awaiting his arrival. His
mother prayed that her husband would come, but her
prayers were seldom answered, and she was the one who
comforted Hayden when he cried.

When Hayden's mother, Catherine, told her husband
that she was pregnant with their second child, he angrily
replied, "I don't want any more children with you. Why
did you let this happen?"

She cried.

"Can't you keep quiet," he shouted at her. "I'm so damn tired of your moods."

And she wept even harder.

"I hope this child is a boy so that I can carry on the family name, because I don't want to be bothered with you after this."

After his rude outburst, she stopped crying. It was as if her tears had finally stopped. Instead, she saw him with a clarity she'd never had before—a very selfish man she didn't like. She quickly left the room, fearful the Lord would punish her for her bad thoughts. A different man might have recognized this as the moment he could salvage his marriage, but Thomas didn't see the sign. Instead, looking at his wife's diminutive figure walking away, he was happy to see her retreat to someplace where she could cry alone.

Seven years earlier, eighteen years old and with child, Catherine had married Thomas V. She became pregnant with Melanie, Hayden's older sister, after surrendering her virginity to him, a man more than ten years her senior; he'd been chasing her since she was fourteen because he was fascinated with her very beautiful face. On his wedding day there was no smile on his lips when he dutifully put a ring on her finger. He was remembering that his father told him he had no other choice, because Catherine came from a very respectable family and he needed to do the honourable thing.

Within a week of marriage, Catherine saw her husband slipping his hands down another woman's thighs and couldn't get the image out of her head. That was the first time Thomas saw her cry all night. After that, whenever he attempted to make love to her, she thought of the other woman and found herself tensing. He got tired of her frigidness and quickly found himself a mistress. A selfish man, he never took the time to learn why his wife couldn't give herself to him willingly and often accused her of being cold. And whenever he had too much to drink, he'd tell her that this was the reason why he seldom turned over to her side of the bed for sexual gratification.

Catherine was truly perplexed when she realized that Thomas didn't want another child. She knew he had no other children, and the few times when she brought up the subject, he never replied to her. She enticed her husband with alluring nightgowns, and he occasionally succumbed, but she never found any satisfaction in his cold thrusts. Whenever she sat on the balcony and looked at her wonderful view, she thought about the rumours from the gossip mongers who gladly talked about her husband's affairs. But she said nothing to him and endured her nights of loneliness. Hayden was the product of a drunken night when he touched her because his mistress was on her period.

When Catherine went into labour, Thomas couldn't be reached so he didn't know when his wife gave birth to his only son. Dr. Hayden Amin was at her side. He held her hand as if she were his wife and wondered,

"Where is her husband?" The doctor knew she was not another abandoned single mother. During his tenure on the island, he felt he'd brought too many babies into the world to desperate young girls who didn't realize that their baby's father had deserted them.

Shortly after meeting Catherine, he discovered that she was the young wife of one of the island's wealthiest men and, despite his professional ethics, developed a deep attraction for her. He didn't understand how her husband could ignore this beautiful, shy woman.

On the day of Hayden's birth, he overheard Catherine's mother say they couldn't find her husband. That's why the doctor decided to stay close to her; he held her hand and instructed her on how to breathe. For eighteen hours Catherine lay on the hard hospital bed with the doctor at her side. Finally, she felt a searing pain and gave birth to a beautiful baby boy with green eyes. Still, her husband was nowhere to be found. No one knew where he was.

As she lay on the bed, exhausted from childbirth, the doctor sat next to her, stroked her head and asked, "What will you name him?"

She appeared very pensive, then looked at him and quietly asked, "What's your name?"

"Dr. Amin," he replied in a puzzled tone.

"I know that. I've been seeing you for several months. What's your first name?"

"Hayden."

He saw she looked confused. "I know it doesn't sound like a name someone from India would have, but my father named me after an Englishman who was very kind to him."

"I like that, and I will name my son after you. You've been so kind to me. I only hope my son will grow up to be thoughtful like you."

"Shouldn't you ask your husband about this?"

Turning her head away, she didn't answer. Just as Dr. Amin was about to ask her if she was sure she wanted to do this, Catherine's mother came into the room, rushing to her grandson's side.

Later that day, alone with her newborn, Catherine held his small, sweet body close to her and knew she didn't want another Thomas in her life; the thought filled her with repugnance. As she held her baby, she looked lovingly at him and whispered, "You're not going to carry your father's name. I don't want you to be a selfish man like him. You will have your own identity, and that's why I'm not calling you Thomas."

Hayden's grandfather was the first on his paternal side see him. He was truly excited when he saw that his new grandson inherited the family's distinct aqua eyes, and that's when he learned that his son hadn't seen the baby. He shocked Catherine by openly showing his displeasure—quickly excusing himself from the room. A few hours later, Hayden's father finally strolled into the hospital. Before he could see his son, his father pulled him aside, reminding him that family is the centrepiece of life. But Hayden's father looked angrily into his father's eyes. "You forced me to marry her because she was pregnant. I didn't want any more kids, because I was going to divorce her when Melanie is big enough to understand. Then she gets pregnant. Now I'm stuck with her."

"Son, Catherine is a beautiful woman from a good family. You're not giving this marriage a chance. Think about what you're doing. This isn't only affecting her. It will impact your children."

"I don't love her. I married her because you told me I had to."

"Don't say that."

"You don't have a bad marriage, so you don't know what it's like. And to make things worse, Catherine's just so damn moody."

"All women are temperamental. You just learn to live with it. I adjusted to your mother's ways. Grow up and be a man. Have you ever thought about what your actions are doing to her? I brought you up to do better than this."

At that moment the little baby boy cried, and his father went into the room. The newborn opened his tiny aqua eyes, the same shade as his father; Thomas felt a surge of emotion that made him temporarily dizzy. In his emotional state, he impulsively went to his wife and kissed her lovingly on her lips. She was so shocked she didn't know what to say or do. For the first time in their marriage, he felt close to her. He was so entranced with his son that he stayed up all night and looked at the baby lying in the crib with adoration. His wife was astonished to see him behave like this and wondered if she should call the child Thomas. But Catherine didn't have time to rethink her decision. Her husband's fascination was temporary, like a passing cloud. Three days later, he left one evening to attend to his mistress' needs and didn't return until the next morning.

She kept the secret of Hayden's name from Thomas until the christening ceremony, where he learned that his only son didn't carry his first name. He was so incensed that he yelled loudly at her in front of the priest and all the people in the church. He was deeply enraged that his firstborn son was the first male child in his family in five generations not to carry the first name Thomas.

That night, he moved into a separate room. Catherine experienced many emotions but wasn't sure if they were happiness or relief. This relocation stopped the irregular intimacy they'd shared. For a very long time, she'd known he spent most of his nights at his mistress', and she finally admitted to herself that she was genuinely thankful she didn't have to sleep with him, because she found the sexual act repugnant.

Despite their mutual dislike of each other, Catherine and her husband kept up a wonderful charade—hosting lavish parties where their guests danced on their balcony and watched the sun rise. Whenever she, her husband and their children left their exquisite home for a social event, they looked like a picture of perfection, with their good looks and perfect manners. But they lived on a small island. Everyone was aware it was a pretence.

Being the social stalwart, Catherine was thankful she'd captured a man from a good family and they had two healthy children. This gave her not just a sense of completeness, but also a belief in her superiority. She pitied his mistress because she knew he'd never leave his family. Her time was spent with her children and her devotion to her God. During the day her friends and family visited her, yet she experienced a deep void and tried to pretend that it wasn't there.

Whenever her friends got together for an afternoon bridge game, the women talked openly about their sex life, but she never participated. Around the bridge table, she was shocked to discover that their nights were filled with heated kisses and deep moans—of hunger, delight and satisfaction; of waking with a body wrapped into theirs. Each time she heard someone say that sex was enjoyable or that she was tired from a night of passionate lovemaking, she realized there was more than the detached humping she experienced with her husband. Not one to break her marital vows, she refused to find a lover to discover what she was missing. At night, as she lay in her bed alone, her body throbbed with unfulfilled desire and she forgot that sex was a sin.

During these times when she wondered what it'd feel like to have the touch of a man, she'd take off her clothes and go to the mirror. Her nude image said many things—her face was still beautiful and her body had enticing curves. At first, she slowly caressed her breasts, till her nipples became firm. As she grew more confident with her touch, her hands moved down, and she touched the rise and fall of her abdomen. With time, she became bolder and let her hands touch between her thighs. In the beginning, she was surprised when she discovered the wetness between her legs—and removed her hands in shock. Intrigued, she knew there was more to discover, and she closed her eyes as her fingers explored this mystery. After she experienced her first orgasm, she lay on her bed dazed and stared at the roof for a long time. There, in the quietness of the room that her husband never visited, she realized there was so much more to her sexuality. That's when she finally cried about the fate of her loveless marriage.

Hayden spent his childhood roaming the land on the hill that the first Thomas fell in love with many generations ago, wholly oblivious to his parent's marital woes. This large playground was lonesome but fed his vivid imagination. Hayden believed he owned a kingdom and below him lived his serfs, over whom his rule prevailed. He often pretended to be Robinson Crusoe, and sometimes he'd invite his sister to be Friday, but with a seven-year age gap, they didn't become friends. His favourite game was Christopher Columbus, in which he imagined he arrived by boat to an uncharted land. As he roamed that hill, filled with the anticipation that the real Columbus probably experienced when he first came to the Caribbean, he was truly happy.

He also played treasure hunt with his best friend, Shaun. Together they buried bottles filled with stones, marbles, balls and small toys. When they returned a few weeks later to recover a bottle, they'd never find it. So they believed that someone had found and stolen their treasures. This often led them to conclude they needed to find better hiding places.

Together these two young boys grew from the boyhood-pranks stage into adolescence, with zeal and curiosity about the opposite sex. Whenever they learned some new tidbit about the female anatomy or the sexual act, they'd gloss over the details, preparing themselves for the future prowl.

Like all teenage boys, Hayden had an unrelenting inquisitiveness about sex and, being a pretty boy, was initiated into the art of lovemaking early—with Dorothy, who was twenty years older. She had been amused when he followed her around his family home, his eyes bulging with admiration for her well-rounded bottom. Dorothy cornered him in the hallway, put his hand on her bottom, and quietly invited him to her home on an afternoon when her husband wasn't around. That afternoon was very satisfying for the two of them and led to another. And soon, Hayden was sneaking into her home whenever her husband was away. On her bed, she guided his hands to the places that gave her the most pleasure. She got a thrill from schooling him about a woman's body and how to please her.

But this woman was not Hayden's only sexual encounter. Soon other women smiled enticingly at him, making it clear they wanted him. It took him a while to understand the impact of his physical appeal. With broad shoulders and strong, muscular arms, Hayden inherited his father's good looks and strong masculine aura. His complexion held the sun's rays, allowing him to shine like a bronzed statue. From an early age, Hayden's mother enrolled him in tennis lessons, which he played avidly, allowing his body to develop the sleekness of an athlete. He walked with confidence that was due to his athleticism and moneyed background. The graceful line that flowed to his shoulders made many women curious to discover what lay beyond his physicality. As they turned their heads in unabashed admiration, he rewarded their attention with a smile that told them he was willing to play.

As he grew up, Hayden watched his father touch other women in places he knew was not right. He also knew his mother knew but ignored it. He'd seen many women with his father. On the small island his father's indulgence was often the topic of the latest gossip. Hayden's mother kept a list in her desk. He saw her sit there dutifully adding new names.

With time, Hayden's elder sister, Melanie, left the island to continue her education. In the quiet house, Catherine's thoughts plagued her. She worried about her only son, fearing he'd grow up to be like her husband. As Hayden left behind childhood, Catherine attended church on a more regular basis, sometimes twice a day, expecting it to soothe her mind. She prayed that as a man her son wouldn't behave like his father; she desperately needed to believe that she'd exorcised those demons from him. In the stillness of the solid pews in the Anglican cathedral, her unhappiness was silenced, and her God told her that only the good suffer. She believed Him, having no one else to trust.

As Hayden moved into manhood, like most adolescents he spread his wings and asserted his independence. He was no longer fascinated by the balcony and walked past it, ignoring the beautiful view his ancestors once enjoyed. The last time he looked at it, he questioned his birth, his parents' indifference to each other, his mother's consuming church addiction, his father's continued absence. Then he turned around and saw that after his sister left the island just as soon as she finished school, wanting desperately to escape her mother's fate, the beautiful house had become a mausoleum.

Hayden's father took him on his Saturday routine, a trip to the rum shop. When Hayden stepped inside, he saw the men playing dominoes and chattering easily amongst themselves. Each man felt he had to relay some wisdom to him. Hayden sat and listened to their beliefs on life and women. They all had a different perspective. He raptly followed a quarrel as the men argued. As the pitch of voices increased, Hayden's father grabbed him— guiding him away from the men. He handed Hayden a beer.

After Hayden's father consumed a few beers and Hayden's head was swimming from his first bottle, his father told his only son, "Forget what all the other men said. The only piece of advice I have for you is to wear your rubber. It saves a lot of hassles. Just take them from the store when you need them. You don't have to ask my permission. I don't want some bastard grandchildren running around the damn island."

"Yes, Dad."

They continued to sip their beers.

"Hayden, have you ever had sex?"

Hayden hesitated before he responded, "Yes, Dad."

His father looked at him respectfully as he took another sip of his beer. "No shit. Don't worry I don't have a problem with that."

"It's occasional," Hayden offered.

"I don't need the details. My son, you're what they refer to as a pretty boy, and there will never be a shortage. Enjoy it. Not every man has it that easy. There are lots of women out there, and they can be so enticing. It can be a lot of fun. Do you have a girlfriend?"

"No."

"One day you will meet someone who makes you want to settle, but don't do it too young. Enjoy yourself. As I've said, they're lots of women out there and there is no need to get tied down too early. Just wear your rubber, so no one catches you until you're ready."

"Yes, Dad."

"We're honourable men in this family. I've built this business much bigger than your grandfather, and I look forward to the day you sit next to me. The island is changing, and there are many new opportunities. We have a great base to ride the future tide and I want you at my side."

"Yes, Dad."

"Your grandfather had integrity and vision. He told me those are the principles for running a successful business. I tell you that now because when you finish school, you will go away to university, like all the men in our family. Your grandfather and I went to business school in London. I want you to go there. They'll teach you new ideas. A whole new world will open up to you, not only academically but also with women. Enjoy that period of your life, because you'll be far from the island and no one will hear about anything that you do."

That night, Hayden saw a side of his father he never knew existed. He observed the ease with which he moved amongst his peers. He heard his deep laughter, which came from his soul, when the men told jokes, and saw the creases in the cracks of his eyes that he never knew existed. This man was different from the sombre man who walked around their home with heavy footsteps.

When Hayden got older, he often reflected upon that night; it was the first time his father revealed himself. In fact, that night built a bridge between the two. In this rum shop, with a few beers in his system, Hayden believed he'd entered manhood.

After that night, he and his father occasionally met at the rum shop. They shared a beer or two and talked about sports and politics. One such day Hayden rose after an hour, saying he had to go.

His father asked, "Why are you leaving so early? It's not even six o'clock."

"I'm going over to my girlfriend."

"I didn't know you had a girlfriend."

"Yes, Dad, we've been seeing each other for a while," Hayden replied.

"Who are her parents?"

"I don't think you know them."

"I know everyone on the island."

"Her name is Kai Robbins."

"Which Robbins is she? Who is her father?"

"She never speaks of him because she doesn't know him. He disappeared when she was a baby."

There was silence. A very heavy silence. Hayden's father now knew all he needed to know.

"Hayden, I didn't bring you up to meet some bastard girl. She's okay for sex, but don't call her your girlfriend."

"Dad, Kai is my girlfriend, and I don't like you talking about her like this. So what if she comes from a poor side of the island? That doesn't mean she isn't a good person."

"Slow down, Hayden. I don't want us to fight over this Kai girl. I have lots of advice for you because I'm older and I've already lived my life. There are always other women. You don't need to get involved so young. You've got to think of your education first; then you can worry about what's-her-name."

Surprising himself, Hayden replied, "Daddy, I'm not you. I don't need a new woman every week. The last thing

I want is to be you. I don't want my wife to have a list, hidden in a desk, of women that keeps getting longer."

There was a long silence. His father's hand shook. The ice in his drink hit the glass, causing it to clink. When he realized what an annoying sound it made, he took a swig of the remaining liquid and slammed the glass on the table.

"Hayden, you don't understand the relationship between your mother and me. Maybe when you're older, you'll grasp what I'm saying, but right now you haven't lived enough to understand . . ."

"There's no excuse. There never has been. You never once considered her or how it affected me or Melanie. Do you know what it's like to walk around that grand house and feel nothing but its unhappiness?"

His father was stunned but didn't reply.

"You *don't* know, do you? I've got to go. Kai is waiting for me."

Hayden left. Watching his son depart from the rum shop, his father ordered another drink. He drank it quickly. Then he refreshed it. That night, he sat on the stool and drank alone.

CHAPTER FIVE

Red Boy

Hayden smiles whenever I read him a story; he marvels at my ability to transform words into a tale, often teasing me that he wants to be my pen when he finishes school. The words I write are the lost stories of the people who once lived on our island. Although I tell him many stories, his favourite folklore is about a man whose power was greater than the night. The first time I read him that story, with each word that left my lips, he looked more deeply at me, fully captivated by my version of this myth:

Not too long ago, at a time when there were more horse carriages than cars, a man named Mervin never went to the bank to deposit the money he made from his business because he kept his wealth on display in his living room, confident that no one dared to steal a penny. Visitors were taunted by a glistening monument of coins and bills adorning his table, but no one ventured close to his pile of money. No one dared to cross Mervin because there were strange and terrifying rumours that he was an all-powerful Obeah man. Seeped in a shroud of mystery, Obeah is a topic rarely spoken of in public. It's a religion that few understand and more fear. Powerful practitioners, like Mervin, are both dreaded and revered.

Mervin was a heavy-set man with dark, brooding eyes. His best friend was a large, black book with leather binding that was always with him. He possessively cradled this book—rumoured to hold the secret to his powers—like a valuable jewel. There were whispers that to protect the key to his Obeah practice, this powerful practitioner had cast a horrible curse on anyone who dared to open his book.

Not many people on the island knew Mervin was a father with an unending devotion to his only offspring, Tabitha.

He loved how her loud, childish laughter created an endless echo of happiness as it bounced off the walls of his home. This child was his unrevealed treasure because he was fully aware what the evil forces would do if they knew of her existence.

Tabitha's mother left him soon after she was born. Mervin seldom thought about her but remembers that he met her when she came seeking his professional services, and while working with her, he had a vision that she'd bear him a child. Using the dark forces that he understood but most people never delved into, he manipulated her mind to go crazy with hot, steamy lust for him. Quickly she was with child.

A few months after giving birth, she was languidly lounging on the bed they shared when she felt a burst of heat. She sat up in shock—smoke was rising from the sheets. Horrified, she quickly jumped off the bed to watch the sheets disintegrate into ash. Yet the mattress remained unscarred. Her blood turned cold, and she hurriedly packed her few belongings.

Fearful that her daughter could carry Mervin's tainted blood, she left her with him.

Tabitha was a light sleeper, and whenever there was a rap on the back door, she woke. She often heard her father's heavy footsteps on the floor and his deep voice speaking to the visitor, but she never made out any words. Sometimes he left with strangers. At other times, he took them into his workroom, a place he'd forbidden her from entering; a place where her father loved to spend lots of time.

One day, as Mervin and Tabitha were sitting at the table, eating lunch, there was a rap. A tall, albino woman stood in the doorway and quietly spoke to him. Mervin became agitated. Without thinking, he rushed out the front door, leaving Tabitha alone. In his rush, he forgot to take his beloved book with him and also left the door to his workroom open. When the precocious Tabitha discovered that she could finally enter the forbidden room, her little feet jumped with glee. Earlier warnings were forgotten as she crossed the threshold into his world.

She was immediately repulsed by a strong, foul odour,

but then the smell changed into a sweet, sweet candy scent. She was no longer repelled as her little feet were seduced to hunt for candy. The child searched the rows and rows of neatly labelled jars that held strange-looking leaves and weird-coloured powders, but couldn't find any candy. Exasperated, she turned around, ready to leave the room, and just as she made this decision, a candy jar magically appeared on the table, where it hadn't been before.

Her childish face lit up as her little feet jumped with delight. Pushing a chair next to the table, she climbed onto the tabletop to get the yummy candy. Once she reached the top, the jar disappeared, and in its place sat a beautifully carved mahogany stand with a large, leather book. The little girl was really puzzled and was about to climb back down to the ground, when she smelt a candy scent emanating from the book, and her fingers were seduced.

Hoping to find the candy, she opened the book but saw only pages of boring handwriting. Disappointed, she tried to close the book but lost control of her fingers as page after page turned, and then magically, the turning stopped. Before her were strange-looking pictures of people wearing odd-looking masks, intriguing her young eyes. Everything appeared misshapen, and as she examined the images, she had an overwhelming urge to laugh. And she couldn't help it when a loud chortle blasted from her lips.

Then she felt a hard slap sting her cheek. She turned, with tears in her eyes, ready to tell her father that she was sorry for disobeying him, but no one was in the room. She looked around. The workroom was empty. Suddenly another slap chastised her next cheek; again she turned to see who was hitting her. That's when she realized she was alone.

The child screamed so loud the shriek carried for miles. Although far away, her father heard her bloodcurdling howl. He saw the smile of deception on the face of the albino woman and the tall, dark man at her side. Saying nothing, he turned and ran as fast as he could. As soon as he got to his house, he went directly to the workroom and saw his daughter's bruised face. She looked at him with fear deeply embedded in her eyes.

He lifted her in his arms and removed her from his workroom; her body felt light and small. He lovingly placed her on her bed. Her young, innocent eyes looked at him through her tears. "Daddy, I'm so sorry. I didn't think I was doing anything wrong. I just wanted to find the candy that you hid. Stop them from hitting me." Then, the hand hit Tabitha, and she screamed, 'Stop this, Daddy. Stop this."

Although Mervin was a man who understood forces that most are afraid of exploring, for once he was helpless. He knew this was not his work and realized the albino woman and her companion had set a trap to get his secrets. Desperate to go to the workroom to see if his powers could undue this curse, he summoned his maid into the room, first ordering her to watch over the child. "Me 'fraid," she said. But he assured her she would come to no harm.

In his workroom the book lay on the floor. He lovingly cradled this large, hard object, seduced by the warmth of the leather—momentarily forgetting it was making his child cry. In the comfort of this room, he forgot about the outside world as he became enticed by its power and its hold on him. Time passed.

He stayed in that room, trying to stop the force that hit his child.

The hands on the clock turned several times before he emerged

from his hiding place, aware that nothing had changed.

He heard the agony of his daughter's cry. As much as he

wanted to go to her, he couldn't. That's when Mervin phoned

the only person he trusted, another Obeah practitioner, an older

woman who had taught him this craft, and pleaded with her to

come to his home. After she saw the state of the child, she looked

pitifully at him. "Things don't look right. What a calamity!"

Then she explained what needed to be done. He shook his head

and told her he would find another way to fix it. The woman

replied, "Don't fight this, my friend. The longer it goes on, the

more damage you're doing to your daughter."

After she left, he returned to his workroom—staying

there all night and well into the day, trying desperately to undo

what was done. But nothing Mervin did worked; the spell was

cast. All he heard was the sound of invisible hands slapping his

beloved daughter.

While Mervin was locked in his workroom, his servant, fearful for the child, wrapped the little girl in a blanket and took her to the hospital. When they realized what was going on, the doctors and nurses were frightened. They didn't go close to inspect her. All they did was point to a bed far from the other patients, where she could scream as loudly as she needed whenever the invisible hands slapped her.

After a few days of hearing the echo of his child's cries in the empty house, the father asked his only friend to come with him to the hospital, where he saw more bruises on his daughter's face. The woman reminded him what needed to be done. Again, he hesitated. Seeing his response, the woman said, "You have no other choice." His head was filled with his child's scream as he replied, "Can you make the arrangement?"

Word was sent, and long after midnight, when the night was at its darkest, a tall, lean man with pointed features and skin blacker than the night knocked at Mervin's door. At his side, the albino woman stood. This man told him they had to wait for a full moon to fix his daughter.

"Do you know the price?" the man asked.

Mervin was quiet for a moment, then nodded. The man turned and walked away, the albino woman following him— both merging into the darkness. The father looked up at the sky. After years of studying the night, he knew the moon would be full in five days.

While he waited, the father sat at his daughter's bedside in the hospital—his beloved leather book in his lap, unopened. Instead, he held tightly onto his treasured book with one hand and his daughter with the other.

On the night of the full moon, the father waited at his house with the book next to him—each tick of the clock, like a loud thump counting time. At fifteen minutes before midnight, the tall man called his name. He held his large leather book very tightly as he followed the man in silence. They climbed a hill, two black souls silhouetted against the landscape that was illuminated by the full moon. Behind them trailed hundreds of stray dogs with droopy tails and skinny bodies. The stranger built a fire. He and the father stood next to it while the dogs watched.

This man spoke into the fire, threw his arms at the wind, and the dogs barked. Then he waved his hands and the dogs ran. It appeared as if madness entered their heads as they ran in a frenzied state, but then they became orderly and began circling the hospital like vultures. Soon a cloud formed in the sky, covering the moon. When the tall stranger threw oddly shaped objects into the fire, the flames jumped into the heavens. They soared, briefly touched the moon and got sucked into the clouds. The dogs howled; the two men chanted and the crickets took up their sound. In the hospital room the invisible hand that hit the child stopped.

Once the child no longer whimpered, the clouds were pulled into the fire and the moonlight returned, casting soft shadows, as if nothing had happened. The man looked at the father. Two sharp brown pairs of eyes penetrated each other. After a moment of hesitation he thrust his treasured book towards the tall, lean man. The lean man greedily grasped it, and the two of them held it for a moment. Mervin looked deeper into the man's eyes, not revealing that he'd cast a very potent curse on the book, one that would cause severe harm to the man. He slowly released his hold. The man greedily grabbed the book and ran down the hill. Mervin watched him, then turned and walked away, slightly bowed. His feet moved quickly until he found himself standing at his daughter's bedside. "Daddy," she cried as he embraced her, "they've stopped hitting me." Mervin bowed his head, unable to look at her. "Yes, my child. I've made sure they'll never hurt you again."

"You're amazing!" Hayden exclaims when I finish. "Where do your stories come from?"

"They blow in the wind," I reply. "You might hear them if you bend into the breeze."

He twists his head to the right. "I don't hear anything." Then he turns his head to the left. An exasperated look comes over his face. "Is this how you do it, because I don't hear a single thing?"

I laugh. "It's there. Believe me, there are thousands of untold stories blowing in the wind. Don't give up. Maybe one day you'll hear them."

Hayden loves my stories, and I read him one story after another. There in my small home, he spends more time with me, forgetting to go back to his grandiose home on the hill. The more time he spends with me, the more he naturally eases into my life.

He meets Ole Bwoy, a thin man in his sixties, who always dresses in a schoolboy's uniform, one Saturday morning when we're walking to the bread shop.

"Morning, Ms. Kai. How you a do?" Ole Bwoy—gazing intently at me—inquires, ignoring Hayden.

His eyes are greedy as he blurts out, "What de word for de day?"

I smile. "Postpone."

"What it mean?"

"To delay or put off until another day."

He looks around for a moment and twists his mouth, "You mean like if it rain and the party have to happen a next day?"

"Ole Bwoy, your head is good. Yes, that's what it means. Now, tell it to me in a sentence."

"The birthday party was postpone till the next day 'cause the rain cause too much mud."

I clap with delight. "You have it. That's right. Great sentence."

There is a big smile on Ole Bwoy's face. "Thanks, Miss Kai. Me go pass by your house tomorrow for a new word unless it rain and me have to postpone seeing you." He nods at Hayden. "You find yourself a good woman. Take good care of she."

Ole Bwoy walks away, mumbling, "Postpone, postpone, to put off until another day."

Hayden looks at me, "What was that about? Is he crazy or what?"

I shake my head. "No, he never went to school and he's trying to catch up."

"What do you mean he didn't go to school? Everyone goes to school. My parents and grandparents did."

"Well, my mother didn't."

"But the school was there. She could have gone."

"Hayden, life isn't always a big house with a pretty view. Not everyone had the chance to go. Ole Bwoy is trying to make up for it now and there's nothing wrong with that."

The air is filled with the tempting aroma of Vee's stewed fish, ripe with the succulent flavours of thyme and garlic. Hayden turns to me. "Kai, your lunch smells good."

My stomach begins to growl in anticipation of the meal. "I'll save you some,"

"Don't bother," Vee shouts. "I heard what y'all said. Hayden, you can stay and eat with us."

A big smile crosses Hayden's face as Vee serves him a steaming plate of fish and the popular Antiguan cornmeal dish fungee. With Hayden's constant presence, Vee has softened towards him, while my mother tolerates him.

Through the corner of her eyes my mother looks at him. "I'm sure that you never ate any fungee, 'cause it poor people food."

Hayden pushes his fork into the steaming yellow ball. "There's so much you don't know about me."

She watches in shock as he devours forkful after forkful. Hayden's eyes are alight with delight. "Vee, you must be the best damn cook on the island. I swear I've never had anything so good. You'd probably make succulent stew from a stone." Then Hayden asks for seconds. Vee refills his plate, and he looks at my mother. "Now you know that this red boy eats fungee."

For the first time since they met, she laughs with him. Just as her chuckle subsides, we're startled by a knock on the door. Standing outside is a man wearing a ludicrous, bright purple hat and purple shoes. He is well known on the island as a staunch supporter of the government and always wears a purple clothing item to openly broadcast support for his political party.

We all sit at the table, and no one gets up. Pretending to ignore him, my mother rolls her eyes.

"Inside," he shouts. No one moves.

"Miss Vee, Miss Sharon, I see you. Please open the door for me, I have an important message for you."

Vee reluctantly gets up, and once he steps inside, he hugs her like a long-lost friend.

"Miss Vee, it's so good of you to invite me in."

"You and us are not friends. She only opened the door because you said you had something important to tell us," my mother replies.

The man ignores her and hands Vee a neatly folded purple T-shirt with his party's name proudly emblazed on it. When she unfolds the shirt, a hundred-dollar bill falls to the ground. My mother hurriedly picks up the shirt and money and throws it at the man. "We don't need this."

"What you mean? Think of this as a thank-you for your vote."

"No one from this house is voting for your party."

"What you mean? They are the best political party in the world. They've done so much for the island. Why you not vote for them?"

"When the white woman ruled the Caribbean, the road in front of my house was not paved. Now the black man in power and still the road not paved. If you ask me, I'd say things get worse because all the roads on this island have too many big potholes. If these politicians did really care about the people and not their pockets, then they would make sure all the roads paved and these potholes are gone. I pay taxes to the Treasury. Where has the money gone?"

"Now, Miss Sharon, don't say that. The government do so much good for the country."

"You lie. All my money goes into the politicians' pocket, and that's why the roads have so many potholes."

"Now, Miss Sharon, what you heard is a pack of lies from the opposition. Look around, Antigua nice. This is the best place in the world. We free. No man own us. What more you want?"

"It's not just about freedom. We all want a decent place to live, with good roads and all this damn thieving to stop. It's like they tell the people it's okay to steal. Every five years, someone from your party knock on me door with a T-shirt and money, begging for my vote. You think I'm fooly or something? I'm going to tell you—and I'll tell anyone else who thinks they can buy my vote—I'm not voting for no damn thief."

The man tries to say something but my mother shouts, "Leave my house. I don't want to see your face 'round here again."

Hayden looks at me in total disbelief. "I can't believe he'd do something like that."

My mother answers, " 'Cause you live up on that hill, you know nothing. What can they buy you that you don't have? This is what I think, if you never met Kai, you would say nothing like this goes on. But worse things than this happen on this island that you don't know about."

The coconut tree stretches gracefully into the sky, swaying peacefully in the breeze. The flamboyant, with its large canopy, is in bloom and its bold flowers light up the island. Whether in a nice neighbourhood or in a poor area, every yard has a hibiscus tree. For the first time, Hayden sees behind this facade and realizes that the extraordinary beauty of the island is a curse, because it seduces you to forget there are problems: our roads have too many potholes, too many children don't have breakfast, the public school system is a disgrace, no one has done anything to make sure that water runs from the pipes, and the politicians are only focused on finding new ways to steal. This is Caribbean life. This is our history. This is what we call freedom.

Hayden and I are together, lying side by side. His body touches mine. It's nighttime. We're looking at the immense sky. With the stars so bright, we feel that if we stretch our hand into the heavens, we can touch them. A shooting star flies across the sky. I make a wish. Hayden also makes a wish. I tell him mine is that I want us to love forever, and I ask him what his is.

"I couldn't think of one. I have more questions than desires." He looks at me, clearly troubled. He confides, "My father expects me to go into the family business—I'm his only son. This is my last year in school, and I'm to leave the island to study, but I don't know how to tell him I don't want to be part of the family business."

"You have to."

"It's not so easy."

"Why?"

"I've been told I must follow in his footsteps. He thinks my interest in architecture is a passing fancy and loves to remind me there are many unemployed architects in this world. All he says is that I just need a business degree because we have a very lucrative family enterprise."

"Hayden, the only calling you have is to be true to you."

"That's your world, not mine. Things are expected of me."

I shake my head, "When my mother realized that I

always came first in class and was skipping grades, she told Vee, "Kai going be a doctor or lawyer. She go make we proud." But I wasn't interested in biology and never thought about becoming a lawyer. She didn't understand why I want to write, when I could do something that'd make more money. I don't know if it was Vee's probing or her own realization, but she finally told me I may never be rich, but my happiness means more than money so I must follow my dream. Hayden, if you really want to be an architect, you need to tell your father."

"My father doesn't know any of this, because he isn't around enough to know how much I love the shape and contours of buildings."

"Go and speak with him. You have to."

"Did you always know you wanted to be a writer?"

There is a moment of silence. I met Hayden when I was fifteen and he was seventeen, and now, for the first time in three years, I hesitate before speaking, because only my mother knows the source of my inspiration.

I was eight years old when the Ancestors told me about the Obeah man—the darkness of the story stayed with me to the evening. I felt the shadows on the wall grow longer and larger. The house appeared darker, and the noises from outside echoed inside. I imagined the shadows jumping to life and an evil force emerging. I shivered and told my mother I was cold. She closed the windows to keep the draft away; still, I didn't feel safe.

At bedtime I pulled the covers up to my neck and for a while slept, then opened my eyes. The room was still dark. All objects were in the right place and nothing had moved. I tried to stay calm but was fearful of closing my eyes. I tossed and turned. Then with my sheet wrapped around me, I sat up on the bed. My mother heard me rustling around and came to my room.

"Kai, you sick?" she asked.

I didn't respond.

She touched my forehead. "You have a fever. I'm going to get something for it." She started to leave the room.

"Don't leave!" I pleaded.

She turned around quickly. "What's bothering you?"

"I'm scared."

"Of what?" Her eyes grew wide with concern.

"A story I heard."

She shook her head knowingly. "You mean them kids at school a talk 'bout Obeah?"

"Uh-huh."

"They are chatting rubbish. Nothing bother you in the night other than your own mind. Kai, nothing out there in the night that not there in the day. Darkness only make you have problems seeing things." She went to the window and pulled the curtain to prove her point. "Look outside. Nothing there but the night. Yes, the sun gone and that's why it dark, but if the sun come back now, everything the same and no one is afraid."

"There is something I never told you," I confessed. "I hear voices that speak in the wind. Yesterday they told me a story that scared me."

"Kai, the only sound you hear is yours, mine or Vee's. We the only people who live here."

"No, this is different. I began hearing this voice when you took me to Montula."

Then I told her the tale about the man, the invisible hands and his child. There was a long pause after I spoke. She stared out the window and mumbled, "He told me that you may hear, but I always thought he was talking rubbish."

"What did you say?"

"Kai, what this voice say?"

"It just tells me stories from long ago."

She stared at the night for a long time and continued to mumble to herself. "I never believed him when he told me."

"What are you saying?"

"Your father was the person who took me to Montula. I was born and lived on this island all my life but never knew about that place. He heard the same voices you hear, but I never believed him. You take after him. All the men in his family hear those voices. You're a girl pickney, so I never thought you'd hear them."

"Are you telling me I inherited this?"

"Uh-huh. You father didn't like those voices. They don't mean you any harm. In fact, your father told me that same story you just told me. Looking back, I should have known where you get your stories."

She kissed my forehead and tucked me into bed. Still

afraid, I didn't want to be alone. "You want me to stay with you?" My mother smiled at me with tenderness.

I nodded and she lay with me on the bed. She fell asleep first. When I no longer felt scared, I went to the window. I looked into the darkness. The moon was full and sat large in the sky. It appeared unreal because of its size. The craters that were created eons ago could be seen by my naked eye. In school they taught me that the moon was dead. As I looked up and saw its size and the light it radiated, I knew it was alive because nothing could be that large and lifeless.

I look into Hayden's eyes, telling him, "As a child, while my mother slept, I'd sneak outside and sit on the steps. Whether it was overcast or a clear night, they were there, telling me stories. I prefer cloudless nights because the sky seems endless as the stars seduce my eyes. Then I'd bend my head into the wind and wait patiently for the Ancestors' voice. They belong to another dimension, one I do not understand. Yet they are very real to me."

He is silent, and for a moment I'm not sure of his response. Then I voice my thought: "Are you wondering if I'm some crazy woman?"

He smiles before he speaks. "I've known you too long to think you're nutty. You're lucky to discover who you are. I've always envied that about you."

"Hayden, when I see you, I see everything I never had. A beautiful home. Money. A family. A father."

"It all looks so pretty from the outside, when it isn't."

"At least you know your lineage. I don't. I've never met my father."

He shakes his head. "I assumed he lived on the island but didn't bother to come and see you."

I explain that I have no memories of this man—he left the island when I was a baby—and that's why it was shocking to learn I inherited this gift from him. That day, I admit to Hayden my deep sadness when I think about my father, because when I touch my flesh and feel its smoothness, I know that half of me is unknown.

Hayden quietly looks at me. "Kai, you're not alone. I don't really know my father, either. Yes, I grew up with him in the house, but he's a stranger. This man doesn't even know his son has a passion for architecture. Even my sister and I are estranged. My home is empty and has been for years."

I put my hands around his neck. "You'll never be alone. I'll always be here."

After Hayden leaves, I think about this inheritance I received from my father. I find it incredible that this gift of hearing the Ancestors can be traced to a line of men and I am the only woman from this bloodline who hears them; yet I allow them to flow through me, enter my pores and filter into my bloodstream so that I breathe and write what they say with more ease than my father or his father.

There are so many questions I want to ask my father about this gift, but he is wandering the world. And there are also other things: I want to know why he forgot about me, but he is a blank sheet; a story that I cannot write; one I will never write. My pen can never describe his face, smile, voice. The sad truth is, if I hadn't attended school and learned about biology, I may have thought my mother dreamed me into existence.

CHAPTER SIX

Change

Hayden and I are at Montula, where the breeze kisses your cheek and tells you stories. He looks on the ground to see if there are any markers to show where people were buried.

"Are you sure this is where it is?" He surveys the rolling hills. "There is only silence and trees."

I nod.

"It can't be," he declares. "Why isn't there an old stump or something to say that this was once a graveyard?"

"Time destroyed everything."

"Then how can you be so sure that this was the burial ground?"

"They've told me."

"I don't hear them speak."

"You never did."

"If this is where the graveyard is, then we need to build a monument so that people like me know that our ancestors lie in these hills."

"That's a great idea. And I also want my own home at Montula, since their voices are so much clearer here."

Hayden takes out a blank piece of paper and begins to draw—handing me the paper when he finishes. "This is my first commission as an architect," he jokes. "This sketch is of your future room." Then he points to a spot on the hill. "I think you should build it there. You'll have a great view."

We are not our usual carefree selves. We haven't been for a while. In two days, Hayden will be leaving to go to university in another country, far from this island, and this thought leaves me with a permanent lump in my throat, like I swallowed a stone.

"What's going to happen to us?" I ask. We've avoided this conversation, and it's here, on this hill, surrounded by the Ancestors, where I have the strength to bring up this topic.

"I don't want things to change," Hayden replies steadily.

"Hayden, this is not a three-week trip. We'll be apart

for months. And it will change us. You could meet someone else."

"There will never be anyone like you. I don't like it when you think like that," Hayden adds.

"But I'm scared that you will forget about me."

"That will never happen. I want us to continue like nothing has changed. We're just apart a few months each year."

I don't respond. He grabs my hand. "Kai, let's just carry on. I can't bear to think about letting you go. I honestly believe that nothing will separate us."

I've grown up on a small island whose shores are bordered by two great bodies of water, the Atlantic Ocean and the Caribbean Sea. If I stand at the shoreline, all I see is water, but on a clear day I can make out the outline of the neighbouring islands like Montserrat, Guadeloupe and St. Kitts. Sometimes those land masses appear so close that it feels like you can take a quick stroll on top of the water for a visit.

Although I've never left this island, I know, with absolute certainty, that the outside world is very different. In the past, Hayden left the island to visit foreign countries, and when he returned, he'd excitedly tell me about vast metropolises filled with bright lights that made it appear as if the world never got dark. I know he is pulled to these lights, and I fear that these foreign places with their magnetic appeal will seduce him to stay, like it has pulled so many from our island. And he'll forget about the sweet stew that we made.

I don't say this to him but think these thoughts. This situation is not one I want to confront, because Hayden and I are in love.

On the day of his departure I awake to the sound of a gentle tap tap on my window. "Kai, wake up! Kai, wake up!" Hayden's voice wraps around me, shakes me from my slumber and pulls me from the bed. I go to the window, where I see him standing outside with an impatient look on his face.

"Get up, Kai. Hurry up! I only have a few hours before the plane leaves. Let's go to the beach."

"I'll be outside in a few minutes," my still-drowsy voice replies.

As we place a blanket on the sand, the sun begins to peek above the horizon. Before us, the serene waves break quietly on the tranquil beach. Grabbing my hand, Hayden tries pulling me into the early-morning water. "Let's go in," he says.

I shake my head. "It's too cold now." But he has a mischievous look on his face as he easily lifts me into his arms and walks towards the water. Once the water reaches his waist, he playfully kisses my lips and tosses me into the sea, like I'm a ball. I scream when I hit the water. He laughs. Once I get my balance, I run quickly to his side and splash the water at him. Unrattled, he pulls me to him, and there, in the quiet of the morning sun, we kiss.

"We're right for each other," he whispers into my ears. "I'll never leave you."

I look into those deep, penetrating eyes that blend into

the colour of the sea and nod, unable to imagine it being any other way. And there, in the morning light, with the gentle waves touching our skin, I wrap my legs around his waist and we seal our love.

Later that day, I try not to show my sadness as I say goodbye to Hayden at the airport. Although his parents are there, they don't acknowledge me; they still treat me like a rotten mango, even though I've been his girlfriend for over three years. Hayden ignores them as we spend all of our time close to each other, like Siamese twins fearful of separation. He wears a bright red shirt and I wear bright red lipstick. When I kiss him, my lipstick leaves red marks that blend into his shirt. I try to remain upbeat, not wanting Hayden to see my anxiety. We speak of nonsensical things as the sun shines on us. The plane looks like a giant bird, with a heavy body and cramped wings. Despite our chatter, we both know our gaiety is fake.

In the midst of our light banter, a muffled voice announces the impending departure. Our bodies move away from each other; a soft breeze blows, separating us. His parents quickly bid him farewell, with his mother clinging to him, reminding him to live within God's footsteps. Just as he goes to give me a final hug, I hand him an empty bottle.

He looks puzzled. "Why are you giving me this?"

"'Cause when you get back, we have to fill it with tamarind stew."

He disappears through the departure gates—smiling—
with the jar in his hands. My eyes are a leaking faucet.
I immediately feel like there is a vast hole inside of me,
because I know Hayden has entered the heart of this
gigantic machine and I don't know what the end product
will be.

When Hayden first leaves the island, I pine for him
and appear inconsolable. My mother, seeing my emotional
state, grabs a mirror and places it in front of me.

"What you see?" she asks.

I reply, "Me."

She shakes her head, "You look in the mirror, but you
don't know who you are without Hayden."

My mother always said that Hayden and I are like
"fungee and pepperpot"—one couldn't do without the
other—and she is right. What to do with my time?
I make lonesome jaunts to the tamarind tree, where
I daydream about him as the day changes to night. I
reminisce about the sound of his voice, and at times I
think I hear him whispering in my ear that he misses me.
I long for the touch of his lips, his breath, his scent.

In this melancholy state I find myself standing at
Montula, looking out from this forgotten hill onto the
scenic landscape, hoping to fill my void. Below me lies
the rise and fall of the hills, and in the distance I see the
piercing blueness of the sea.

I dip my ear into the wind and scream into the silence,
"How does love survive?"

"Kai," they whisper in the wind, "what's your favourite drink?"

"Why do you want to know that?" I ask, puzzled. "What does that have to do with my question?"

"Just answer," they reply.

"Coconut Crush."

"Why?"

"It always tastes good, and it makes me feel wonderful every time I drink it."

"Passion is finite, but love has no boundaries," they answer. "You are just learning about these two emotions; they appear similar yet are so different. When passion dies, you will look at that person and see an empty cup filled with a liquid that you're tired of drinking. But if there is love behind that passion, the cup is inviting and will remain your favourite drink. That is why every time you taste it, you will feel like you're in a place—far from the rest of the world—where you can savour and enjoy its flavour."

Their words don't offer me any comfort, and I ask them to tell me a happy story to make me forget everything. I close my eyes, dip my ear into the wind and wait for them to speak. But there is silence. Frustrated, I reopen my eyes and am shocked to discover I'm no longer standing in a forsaken graveyard that is overgrown with grass and trees; all around me is row after row of neat burial plots.

At first, I think I'm dreaming and rub my eyes. This can't be real. But it is. I'm standing in another time, hundreds of years ago when they buried the dead at

Montula. All around are wooden tombstones and crosses. After the shock wears off, I roam the hill, discovering names like "Teacher Bee" and "Strong Jack." Small phrases salute loved ones: "beloved mother of"; "died running for freedom"; "finally found peace," "in a better place." As I walk, I stumble on a branch and fall onto an old grave. Looking up, I see the name inscribed is "Betsy, Mother of Montula." For many moments I stare at it. Who is Betsy? Why is she Montula's mother?

Hearing movement, I turn around and see a woman preparing to sit next to a grave. As she's not dressed in modern clothing, I know she's from a different era. A hat hides her face as she's in deep conversation with the tombstone.

"Daddy," I overhear, "Happy Birthday. You know I wouldn't forget—I never forget. When I was a little girl, you always made sure I had a cake. And I still bake you one, even though you're not here. When I get home, my husband and I will sing you 'Happy Birthday.' There is so much to tell you. First, I have to say that I'm saddened because people are forgetting about this cemetery that you worked so hard to preserve. Now we free, everyone wants to forget anything that happened when we were slaves. I can't blame them. There is no good to remember.

"Have you seen Mamma? Did she make it safely to the next side? It still hurt me that they sell Mamma. I don't even remember her, but I hope that you found her and the two of you are finally together.

"It has been over five years since emancipation and there have been only small changes on the island. We need so much more. I wish you'd lived to see the day when we were freed and how we danced and danced from night to day—and into the night again. No one was exhausted. How could we be? Our dark skin glistened with sweat as our bodies moved to the beat of the drums and the 'chak-chak' seed pod from the flamboyant tree. My husband and I danced and danced until we felt our feet were going to fall off. Then we went home and made love. I conceived that night. My son was born nine months to that day. Yes, on May first. His name is 'Freedom.' What else could we call him?"

The woman puts the flowers next to the grave and leaves. Once she is gone, I go to the grave where she'd sat and see the name "Miracle Robbins" and the epitaph "The Keeper of Montula."

Who is Miracle? His last name, similar to my own, Robbins, shocks me because with absolute certainty, I'm sure I am his descendant, and I want to know more about this blood line—who was he? I stand there, hoping to hear something of his life, but nothing happens. Time doesn't move again. All that sits in front of me is a marker and name. However, I'm assured that Montula was real, like the flesh on my skin and the blood in my veins.

Brittany and I quietly pass notes to each other in class. She is confiding to me about a problem with her boyfriend, Shaun, Hayden's best friend. Their relationship was inevitable, since Shaun spent a lot of time with Hayden and Brittany was continually around. As she furiously writes about their most recent fight, and they seem to fight on a regular basis, I wonder if what they experience can be labelled love, because she's having more trouble than good times with Shaun. I want her to find someone, but Shaun is not a good man. He is always putting her down and has eyes filled with wanderlust.

For five years, we attended secondary school and sat with our desks side by side. Our curriculum for most of these years was unimaginative, filled with rote repetition of words and regurgitation of facts. My boredom was evident throughout, but in our final year, everything changes, when our new history teacher, Mrs. Taylor, a tall woman with long limbs, who always wears shock-ingly bright red lipstick, becomes our homeroom teacher. Under her tutelage my mind soars.

On the first Friday of the school year, a hot, September day, she sits, looking at the class, and smiles. As I prepare myself to open the tedious history book, she surprises me by going to the blackboard to hang a poster of Lord Nelson. Brittany and I exchange looks in puzzlement, and we are not the only ones. She notes this expression on all twenty-two faces.

Unperturbed, she announces, "Class, close your history books. I think we need to do things differently. It's time to debate what you've learned all these years. I want to hear your voices. Let's talk about Lord Nelson. Look at his picture on the wall—does anyone want to say something about him?"

The class is uncomfortably quiet, unsure of the next step, wondering if this is a trick. I hesitate for a moment, then put up my hand. Mrs. Taylor nods.

"When I see Lord Nelson's picture," I begin, "I see a man who proudly wore his naval uniform. Though his face was well proportioned and pleasing, I'm drawn to his hands—the way they boldly and fiercely clasp his sword; this gesture tells me why he was greatly feared in battle and why he defended Britain with such valiant honour."

She smiles and then asks, "Yes, that's true but what else do you know about Lord Nelson? I'm not going to put down his accomplishments, because he truly deserves a place in British history. But I'm a West Indian, and I see him as one of the people who helped keep a system in place that uprooted millions of people from Africa."

Suddenly there is a silence in the class. No one ever spoke about history in this way; Mrs. Taylor was tackling a taboo topic, something never mentioned in history books or even in school.

In the silent classroom Mrs. Taylor looks at me. "Kai, you were the only one to speak. What do you think?"

"I don`t think it takes away his feats—he was one of the greatest British naval officers."

"I agree. But let`s talk about how this impacted our island. You all know the Caribbean territories were prized possessions for the European powers because sugar was king in the 1700 and 1800s. Do you remember when the

Seven Year War ended in 1763 the French gave up Canada to the British in order to maintain their Caribbean territories? I want to know if Nelson was an abolitionist. Did he own slaves? Was he a product of his time? Did he have the humanity to notice the injustice against people with a different skin pigment?"

Nelson is the first of many historic persons and incidents we debate. During my final year in secondary school, the classroom comes to life on Friday afternoons. At long last, we have a teacher who gives us freedom to forget our robotic recitation of the archaic words in the dull history book. Instead, we realize how all the lines are connected and history is actually a sum of different parts and characters.

The day Mrs. Taylor places a picture of Toussaint Louverture on the blackboard, the entire class comes to life. We all agree that he was great—it was he who led the Haitian Revolution in 1791 when no one thought people with dark skin had moxie. His leadership led to the creation of a nation. My classmates speak with pride about the revolution.

On Fridays, I learn about the many opinions of my classmates, and each week they become more heated.

When we finally speak about William Wilberforce, the British Parliamentarian whose voice led to the abolition of the slave trade in the British colonies, and Olaudah Equiano, a former slave who joined the abolitionist movement in Britain, I freely share my thoughts with everyone: "They were men who never held a dagger or a gun but used their determination to bring about change."

As the school year progresses, my classmates look forward to our Friday treat. In our final month, Mrs. Taylor announces that each student will make a presentation about an historical figure or incident.

For my turn, I place a large, blank sheet on the blackboard and then use crayons to draw the outlines of faces. I tell the class that millions of people never made their way into the history books. However, their quiet deeds of rebellion, when added together, are as destructive a force as the gusts in a hurricane. I describe a slave rebellion that once took place on the island that never made its way into the grey history book. And I happily ask the girls to join me in reciting the leaders' names: King Court, Tomboy, Scipio and Fortune. Others join in, and Mrs. Taylor takes up the chant as our voices carry their names in the cool Antiguan breeze.

For most of my life I wore a beige school uniform and sat in a classroom where I was taught that one plus one equals two, Christopher Columbus's crew sailed on three ships to cross the Atlantic, and tourism is the country's main industry. Whilst this information was important, my reality is that I'm a student of two classrooms: the one of rote memorization and the other of the unseen. The Ancestors fill in the gaps left in the history books and explain why people with my colour are not recorded—as if we were mere footnotes in recorded time. Their school taught me there are different types of history: the told, the untold, the imagined and the real. Through the Ancestors I see and experience a dimension that doesn't exist for most people, and therefore, it is so easy for me to shed my stifling beige uniform.

Hayden returns to the island in the early evening. I'm at the airport. His parents are also at the airport. They don't acknowledge me, but I don't care, I'm so happy. I wear his favourite dress and bright lipstick. Hayden requested I wear those two items. Standing on the balcony that overlooks the runway, I hear the roar of the plane. It appears as a dot and grows into a large machine as it smoothly glides onto the runway. Although there is a flurry of activity once the plane has landed, it seems to take a long time before they finally open the door. Hayden is not amongst the first to disembark, but then I see him and yell his name. Even though he is so far away, the wind carries my voice, and he hears it; he looks up and sees me waving at him from the balcony that overlooks the airport. Although some distance still separates us, he enthusiastically signals and I laugh with happiness.

When he clears customs, I'm the person he runs to. His lips are sweet as he pulls me into him with great fervour. In that moment of passion, my fears about our separation subside. We hold onto each other, fearful of letting go and discovering this is a dream. Then I hear them clear their throats. Hayden keeps his arms encircled around me as he goes to his parents.

They tell Hayden that he has to go with them. He whispers, "Go home and wait for me."

Hayden later tells me that once they are alone, his mother says, "Why did that girl have to be there?" An uneasy silence fills the car. Hayden becomes sullen. For the past year, he didn't have to listen to her badmouthing me, and he's so irritated that he doesn't bother to sit down with his parents when they reach home. Nor does he look at the beautiful view that once fascinated him. Instead, he defiantly drops his suitcase on the floor and grabs his car keys. He runs to his car, desperate to get away from them, and speeds down the hill to me.

We are so consumed by our passion that our clothes are still on when we fall onto the bed. It happens so quickly that our bodies can't recall the moment. Then Hayden's hands reach for me, slowly undoing the buttons on my clothes. At the same time, I remove his clothes with the same unhurried deliberation. Then my hands touch his skin, as if rediscovering the feel of him, like the first time we made stew. Next to my bed sits a bowl of tamarinds. I rub them onto his skin, which easily absorbs its flavour. My mouth touches him, I taste the flavour of the fruit on his skin. That night we don't speak as we reacquaint ourselves with our hungry passion for each other.

It feels like we were only apart for a few days and not several months. We fall back into our passionate routine, and once more our world revolves around each other. We make tamarind stew. We swim in the sea and we dance all night long. I come to terms that this will be our routine for the next few years. With him so close and never leaving my side, I believe that a love like Hayden's and mine is rare and never ends.

CHAPTER SEVEN

'Cause He Name Man

Although the night is dark, with no moon, and the stars are lost behind the clouds, it doesn't dampen our celebratory spirit as Hayden and I are at a party with Brittany and Shaun. The four of us forget time, dancing gleefully to the latest calypso music. The night spills into the early hours of the new day. The deejay slows down the music to a background hum as small cliques form— chatter and laughter fill the air. Brittany and I leave the men to catch up with some friends. On our way back we notice Hayden and Shaun are deep in conversation, oblivious to everyone.

We smile mischievously, quietly sneaking up on them, fully aware they don't realize our proximity. Hayden is talking in a quiet tone to Shaun.

Brittany and I overhear him saying, "Shaun, my father once told me that there are plenty of women out there, and it's so true. In those big counties no one knows you, and I can do what I want. It's so easy to have more than one girlfriend, and Kai has no idea about what I'm doing. Although I have a problem because one of them insists on visiting me, I've lied and told her my father is sick. Hopefully that will keep her away. How the hell would I explain that to Kai?" Then he adds, "I hate to say this, but I have some of my father's traits."

Shaun laughs in agreement. "Yes, you are your father's son—crapaud don't jump and its pickney walk." (Frogs don't jump and its children walk)

I dig my hand deep into Brittany's flesh, and she yelps in pain. They turn. For a moment, Hayden thinks I'm ill—I look ashen—but as he makes his way to me, I shake my head and put up my hands, creating a wall. I yell, "Don't you come near me. Just stay away. *Who are you?*"

Suddenly realizing I overheard him, he screams my name, but the sound flies into the air, finding no receptacle. The four of us are standing there, dumbfounded. Although the sun is beginning to rise, the new day feels like night.

Brittany intervenes: "Hayden, leave her alone."

"Kai, I've got to speak with you"—his voice is barely a squeak, his face twisted in shame.

"No, you won't." Brittany's speaks for me, her voice firm.

"This is between me and Kai. I love Kai. Let me explain."

"Hayden, you have a funny way of showing it. I can't blame her for not wanting to talk with you." Brittany replies as she grabs my hand.

Hayden watches helplessly as she takes me away from him. I am numb. There are no words inside of me. I'm only aware of the cold space.

I remember getting home and closing the door to my room. I stay there for a long time, fearful of leaving its comfort; cushioned only by my arms wrapped around my body and four impenetrable walls. In the quiet of this room, I feel a tear slide from my eyes; one drip becomes a second drip, then a third. They come out, one by one, slowly and painstakingly forming a small stream on my face that ends in a puddle on my shirt that eventually makes a large, wet patch.

When he comes to our front door a few days later and I announce that he isn't welcome anymore, my mother and Vee realize that Hayden and I had a fight. At first, they assume it's a lover's quarrel, but they realize it is something more when one day grows into two days, then a week. During this time, Hayden's car is parked outside our house, patiently waiting for me.

Day after day, Hayden is there with the sun browning his skin, hoping I will come to him, but I've retreated into my small bedroom; hoping these walls are strong enough to hold my pain. Brittany visits me. She holds my hand, but I just sit there and look at her—still unable to talk about it. Though I know the Ancestors are there, I can't even bend my head into the wind.

One day my mother, tired of seeing Hayden sitting mournfully by himself, looks at Vee and says, "I'm going to talk some sense into that red boy's head. This is pure nonsense."

The front door opens, and Hayden looks hopeful, but then sheer disappointment spreads over his face when he sees my mother. She asks him to join her. The two of them sit uncomfortably on the balcony. After an uneasy silence she finally speaks.

"Now, Hayden, I know you do something to vex Kai," she begins. "I don't care what you did—that is your business—but this much I know about life: when a woman vex, she vex, and she don't stop being vex very easy."

"I want to talk with her. I need to explain things."

"Hayden, from the way she's behaving, I know you did she wrong and a big one at that. What you expect? She'll just hug you and say love will fix this? Things don't work that way."

"What do you know about male and female relation-ships?" he angrily asks her.

My mother shakes her head and calmly responds, "Hayden, let me tell you something. I never pretended to fancy you when you first walked through this door. You see, I used to clean houses of people like you, and me know things about your kind of people. I said to myself, this red boy here for no good 'cause I know that most of y'all people think them better than me. But you treat Kai good, and that all I really cared about. Now you're on your high horse, talking like you know everything in the world 'cause you're a man. I've told you the first lesson earlier, and you know how come I know that?

"Life taught me that love's not easy for it's between two different people, whether it's man or woman. I once lived with a man, so I know about man. This thing between two people not so crazy, but everyone make it so. Yes, I love a woman. So what? It's all the same. You see, two people are two different people, whether they are a man or a woman. But Vee and I decided we don't need that kinda botheration to make things work. We long time learn that if we want to stick together, we have to stand as one. If Kai father knew that, then maybe he would be in this house and not Vee."

Then my mother angrily stands up. Hayden shifts uncomfortably in his seat. "I'm sorry," he mutters. "I didn't mean to insult you."

But my mother looks at him, loudly sucks her teeth and walks inside. She says to Vee, "It's 'cause he name man. Only a man can do something bad to a woman and think he can get away with it. That's the way man behave all the time. Worst yet is that him believe that him right and the world wrong him when he do wrong. I really don't know why woman bother with man."

Hayden hadn't been around for a while and I go outside and sit on the balcony. I am easing into the comfort of the cushions in the seat when I hear Hayden's voice.

"Hi."

I stare blankly at him. Now that he's standing in front of me, I truly know that I really don't want to see him. In his hands is a bag of tamarinds. He tentatively sits next to me and begins peeling them. I watch him shell the tamarinds and put them into a lifeless bowl, but I don't help him. As his hands move, I remember the closeness we'd shared, and I hate to think his hands touched someone's flesh with the same intimacy I'd known. I can't imagine that someone else has lain with him and shared his kisses. He's nervous, and it takes him a long time to remove the soft casings of the fruit. When he finishes, he looks at me, "The stew always brought us back to each other, but we are so much more than tamarind stew. I just miss you."

I instinctively look deeply into his eyes. For a second, I'm lost in his sea of helplessness, but I turn away. Then defiantly picking up the bowl, I throw the tamarinds into the yard. Flying into the air, they land in the dirt, their brown colour melting into the colour of the soil. Hayden calmly gets up, picks each one from the ground and puts them in the bowl. He comes back to where I sit and rests the container next to me. I pick up one tamarind and I throw it. I repeat this gesture again and again. With each throw, my arm becomes stronger, until the tamarinds fly

past the fence and reach the street. A stray dog, watches
the road being pelted with a thin brown fruit, gets up
from its resting place behind a rusting car to investigate.
The dog lazily sniffs the tamarinds and then walks away;
I start to cry. Hayden pulls me to him, feeling my tears;
I feel his tears, but I untangle myself from him and push
him away.

I yell, "You lied to me. How can I ever trust you again?
Leave me alone. You always said there was no one else."
Then I run inside and leave him.

Hayden doesn't contact me until the day he leaves the
island. On the way to the airport his car pulls up outside
my home; his suitcase sits on the backseat, like a forlorn
passenger. When I see him, I get up from the balcony and
make my way inside. He quickly runs to the door, only
to get there as it slams shut in his face. He stands outside
while I stand inside. Both of our bodies are pressed to the
door. The wood separates us. It is hard and cold. Through
the door he tells me that he hopes we can find our way
back to each other. And Hayden reminds me that there is
a bond so deep between us that even if we don't speak or
see each other, we are still together. Then he gets into his
car and drives away.

His words come back to me again and again. By that
time in our lives, we are more than two teenagers who
discovered sexual passion together. Yes, we'd explored the
thrill of intimacy, and there were nights when I lay awake
with excitement as I relived the flame of our bodies, but

there was so much more to us. When I first made love
with Hayden, he promised me he'd never hurt me. He
confided that he never wanted to be like his father. His
greatest fear was to make a woman cry as much as his
mother. He shared with me the names of his father's
conquests, and he believed his acts caused his mother to
become a servant to her Bible. I understand that when
Hayden saw me cry, it hurt him. I know the man who is
Hayden, who deep in his heart hates breaking
any promise.

Not till we go to Montula do I confess the depth of
my heartbreak to Brittany. As we look out at the open
fields, I confide that I heard an explosion when Hayden
spoke those words of betrayal, and it left me deaf. My
voice carries in the wind at Montula, resting safely with
Brittany and the Ancestors. It is soothing to finally reveal
these emotions that are buried inside of me. After I finish
speaking, Brittany and I say little. We sit and look at
the hills.

As the sun begins its descent Brittany leaves to meet
Shaun, but I have another friend whom I'd neglected.
I sit alone at Montula, with no one around me on that
beautiful, sloping hillside, and dip my head into the wind.
Their voice rises to the cadence of the landscape, soft and
calming. And there, on that lonely hill, I close my eyes
and they comfort me with a refrain:

In the light of the morn

our ghosts cry in the dawn

Anointed with tears

they beseech us to embrace

The hour clock stops

The sound is deafening

Time, we bemoan

Lost years, sacrificed union

From our point of departure

we stare at the holes

Nights of futile reminiscence

lips left unkissed

Questions never spoken

whys left hanging

Will you finally answer

They tell me there are different ways to express the pain of love gone astray. Sometimes someone writes about their debilitation while others express sorrow differently. That is why history is filled with eloquent sonnets by people who cried, and they further soothe me with a story.

"Rebecca, fair and true . . . Rebecca, smile and don't be blue."

As a child, Rebecca never smiled, so her caregiver created a nursery rhyme about her. When she asked who made it up, the woman who cared for Rebecca said it was her mother. But the little girl couldn't remember her mother. Nor did she even know her father. It was as if she were a plant that sprang up on the plantation—one day a seed in the soil and the next day, a vine growing in the ground.

Whenever she asked about her parents, she was told she was a miracle, because God gave birth to her without a mother and father, and this made her God's special gift to the world. As a child, Rebecca truly believed she was extraordinary. By the time she was twelve, she realized that there are no special children, and they were told tales like this to hide an ugly truth.

Not only was her skin colour several shades lighter than all the other slaves, but she sported a head full of ringlets that all the other women enjoyed combing. "That girl have good hair," they said as they put the comb through it. "See how the comb slide like a knife through butter."

Life was unhappiness—revolving around hard, debilitating work from one day to another. Rebecca never had the chance to savour the sound of the whistling wind, and her face only knew how to scowl. This changed when Kwami came to the plantation. Rebecca noticed him because he was proud; he never showed fear. That's why when Kwami looked into her eyes, for the first time in her life she smiled, and an emotion surfaced that she'd never known existed: it was called hope.

Kwami came to her bed each night, and every morning she awoke with a smile; Rebecca glowed for the first time in her life. One night he confided that though the sugar cane grew to great heights and the soil was very fertile, he didn't love this land. From sunup till sundown, year after year, he'd worked in those fields. He compared the blackness of the soil to his own skin; they were both a machine for another man. He took no pride in the harvest, and when he hacked at the cane, his rage made him hit the cutlass so hard that sometimes the instrument broke.

At night as they lay together, their limbs tightly wo-ven into each other, Kwami whispered that he heard of a place called Freedom's Point, and when the time was right, they'd escape. Finally, they'd be free to love and have children. He told her that although the land was beautiful with tall palm trees that swayed in the gentle breeze and rolling hills lush with vegetation, he couldn't appreciate it, because he was not free.

With Kwami in her life, Rebecca forgot that there were devils around. And in her world, one devil was named the overseer. The dark people were familiar with his frequent visits to the slave quarters, where he brazenly grabbed any woman of his choosing.

One night he climbed into Rebecca's bed and savagely pried open her legs. She was unable to stop this beast as he tore at her body. The man whom she loved heard her screams but was helpless to stop the act. That night, she experienced savage-ry as blood poured from between her legs. The overseer bit her, slapped her, and then he walked away from her battered body.

After he left, Kwami sat in a corner and sobbed. Her

solace came from the other women, who held her bruised body.

After that incident, Kwami never touched her again; rather, he

turned his head the other way whenever he saw her.

Once the overseer had his way with Rebecca, he contin-

ued to visit. She was helpless as he vilified her body. The scowl

returned to her face—Rebecca forgot how to smile. When she

discovered she was pregnant, she felt no delight that a life was

growing inside of her. She decided to end her life. With steely

determination, she placed a knife under her mattress. Her plan

was to plunge it into her heart when everyone was asleep. That

night, as the overseer pushed himself into her, Rebecca felt the

knife. Her anger and hatred led her to grip it and thrust it into

him with the same force and vigour as his unwelcomed thrusts.

The knife easily found an opening, and he only had a short time

to realize her act before he died. She lay there, pinned to the bed

by his lifeless body—his bright red blood, spilling onto her.

The quiet in the slave quarters said something was not

right. A woman came to her and saw blood oozing from the

overseer's body, with Rebecca lying underneath him, alive. She screamed and soon a group of people gathered around her, look-ing at the lifeless body of the pale man lying on top of her. Then Rebecca felt someone throw his body aside. She looked up and it was Kwami. She sobbed when she finally felt the comfort of his embrace.

"Them go kill you," someone said. "And they won't show no mercy 'cause they go torture you to death."

Then another person grabbed her. "Run, Rebecca, run. Don't look back. Don't stop running even when you think there's no road—one is there. Just keep one foot moving in front of the other. You know when you find the right place 'cause your feet can't go no more."

Kwami grabbed her hand. "We will go to Freedom's Point."

"Where is it?"

"We go follow the road they tell me about."

Together they ran. The night was dark, with no moon,

but their eyes quickly adjusted. They found their way through the rough terrain. After they'd run some distance and looked back, they heard the commotion at the slave quarters and knew that someone other than the slaves had discovered the body. They didn't care, because they were on their way to freedom.

Their legs moved quickly, taking them away from the slave barracks. In the distance they heard horses galloping fast, dogs barking, and knew they'd picked up their scent. They weren't scared; freedom was close.

The path became scragglier. Still they followed the over-grown track that led uphill. The sound of water became stronger and louder. Then the two lovers stopped. They were standing at the edge of a cliff. Below them the sea violently met the land. The moon was beginning to rise, and they saw its beams on the ocean for the first time. Despite the craziness of the moment, they stopped to admire its absolute serenity. They'd never been allowed to savour these moments.

The sound of the dogs pierced their milieu. In the distance they saw a wagon, people, chains and guns, and for once they didn't feel fear. They looked at each other. No need for words.

Standing at the precipice they heard the water hit the cliff. In

the sweet intoxication of their first moment of freedom, they

remembered, "Run, run, run. Don't look back. Don't stop run-

ning even when you think there is no road. There is one. Just

keep running. You'll know when you there 'cause you'll finally

know freedom."

Together, with their hands clasped, they ran. Around

them, the darkness felt like a salve. High in the sky the moon

provided light. This time their legs didn't stop when they reached

the cliff. Their hands remained clasped as their bodies fell freely

when the earth was gone. They marvelled at its lightness and,

for a moment, felt as if they were gliding. When their bodies

hit the water, they closed their eyes as the water softly embraced

them. Their bodies floated for a few moments and then glided

slowly to the bottom of the sea, resting on the reef next to the

other corpses. Here, the fish swam and feasted, their brilliant

colours a sharp contrast to the brown of the reef.

Stories have always soothed me. My life is intertwined

with them. The story of Rebecca and Kwami was another story reminding me of the direction of my life. I'd finally graduated from school and held a diploma in my hand. As I stand on this hill and say goodbye to the love I'd shared with Hayden, I knew where my life would take me.

I tell my mother and Vee the story. Their faces are captivated by Rebecca and Kwami, and that's when I tell them my plan.

I say, "Now that I'm nineteen and completed school, I don't want to get a job right now. I want to follow my dreams and write a book of short stories first. Are you okay with this?"

There is a moment of silence. Neither Vee nor my mother looks at each other or at me.

"Why you want to write a book, when you can get a job?" my mother asks.

"It even sounds strange to me, but I know this is what I need to do. I'm asking for your support. Give me this chance."

"Tell you what," my mother replies. "We go give you a year to figure out what you want to do, but you go have to help us in the store. Vee, what you think?"

"I never once thought Kai would do things normally, so I agree. The store doing well, so let us make sure our child gets a chance to live her dream. Kai, write your book, and let's see how things turn out."

That is how I come to stay up late many nights,

turning the words of the Ancestors into a book. Time blurs as I write and rewrite their words. The months pass, and as I am completing my last story in the anthology, I awake to sobs.

I leave my bedroom to investigate where the sound comes from. My mother isn't around, but Vee is sitting on the couch, softly crying. I sit next to her and wonder what has upset my usually calm stepmother.

"What's bothering you, Vee?" I pry.

She doesn't speak and cries even harder. I wrap my arms around her. She rests easily into me, and since we don't move, we are like a statue of two women frozen in a hug.

"My father died," she finally confesses.

"I'm sorry," I respond. I'm a bit puzzled because although I've lived with Vee most of my life, I can't remember her mentioning her father. That morning I learn about her life before coming to Antigua. Born in St. Lucia, she was her parent's last child and only girl. They enjoyed dressing her in frilly dresses and placing colourful ribbons in her hair. Never liking all that fuss, she pulled out the ribbons and tore off the frills—always upsetting her father.

Her mother died before she turned six, and her father never remarried. At Christmas and birthdays he bought her dolls, which she put aside in favour of cars. For a long time, her father told himself his daughter rejected these feminine wiles because she had too many brothers and was not in touch with her girlish side.

When Vee developed breasts, she showed no interest in boys. However, her father told himself it was her strong Christian values that kept her from veering off the straight and narrow path. When his only daughter insisted on cutting her hair short like a boy, he accepted that because he instinctively knew men don't like women with short hair and he wouldn't have to worry about the scourge of an illegitimate grandchild.

As a preacher, Vee's father spent a large portion of his time dissecting the lives of the people in the community. Well versed in the Bible, he memorized many passages, using his knowledge to remind people that his God of fire and brimstone judged them if they strayed. There was no leniency when he quoted from the Bible about the disgrace the unmarried, pregnant teenage girl caused her family. Whenever he passed an adulterer, whether at church or walking on the streets, he'd open his Bible in front of their face and spew out the word of God to show his wrath at their sinfulness.

This man felt totally betrayed when his daughter innocently revealed she wouldn't know how to love a man but her eyes shone whenever she saw a woman. Those words enraged Vee's father; forgetting the Bible said that we must love everyone, he violently grabbed that Holy Book and thrust it in his child's face. Vee stepped back in fear, but her father forcefully pushed her on the chair and screamed the passages that condemned his daughter to hell because her thoughts were an abomination to God. Then he took Vee to the altar and sought a purification of her soul. After hours of this ritual, his daughter remained the same. As much as he assessed and reassessed it, he knew there was only one choice. The teachings that he believed told him to reject his only daughter because she couldn't love a man.

He did the only thing that'd save his family from this shame—bought her a one-way ticket to Antigua. At the airport he told her, *don't return unless you repent your ways.*

"All these years, we never spoke. I always hoped he would want to make peace, but that won't happen now."

Vee continues crying, and when she controls herself, she looks me directly in the eye. "Kai, every Christmas morning, the day of the Lord's birth, I called him. When he heard me on the line, he always hung up. I know that he believed in his Bible, but I am no sinner. I never killed anyone. Not once did I ever steal anything from another soul. I've been a good mate to your mother. Since I was born, he always said the Bible tells us to be good people and a good neighbour. I've been all that and more. It's such a shame that I could never share my happiness with my family!"

The following morning, a very distraught Vee boards a plane to St. Lucia for her father's funeral. The previous day, after over twenty years, she speaks with her eldest brother, who tells her she must come home for the funeral. He assures her he needs his only sister at his side when they bury their father. Then he cries when he tells her that they shouldn't have lost all this time.

After Vee boards the flight, my mother and I drive

directly to the store. The bakery is no longer solely a
pick-up operation. Now we have some seats and tables.
The four cakes on the original menu are still there, but
now we offer over ten different cakes, along with a variety
of desserts and tasty snacks.

Each day before the sun rises, my mother and Vee
would leave their bed and make their way to the store.
In the early morning hours, they beat butter and sugar,
knead dough and whisk eggs. While some customers
still only pick up their order, now a new clientele hangs
around and munches on the goodies.

I've always assisted at the front counter because
Vee realizes that my mother doesn't like dealing with
customers; her razor-sharp tongue is not always good
for the business. In Vee's absence, my mother is forced to
work the front counter a little more. She tries to smile, but
as the day wears on, I notice she gets more irritated. That
afternoon, when a new customer comes through the door,
his eyes sparkle when he sees my mother. She ignores his
obvious stare and asks what he wants; he mischievously
replies that he wants a woman like her, sweet of face and
sexy of body. Then he adds that although he'd heard that
this place makes the best cakes, no one told him about the
sweet woman behind the counter.

My mother looks at him through the corner of her
eyes. "How many other woman you say this stupidness
to?" Then she sucks her teeth so loudly that everyone
looks at the man and laughs. Without purchasing
anything he quickly leaves the store.

I chuckle for the rest of the afternoon whenever I remember the look of embarrassment on his face. My mother is a very attractive woman, and men who are unaware of her relationship with Vee often give her admiring glances, but she never smiles back. When I tease her about the incident, she glares at me. After she closes the shop, she cuts a healthy piece of coconut cake and places it on two plates—motioning for me to join her.

"Lawd, me tired. Kai, let's just sit down and relax. We need to forget about the day," she says, putting her fork into the cake.

"It's my favourite," I reply. I put a forkful in my mouth.

"Me weary," she adds. "And I miss Vee bad bad bad. Things are easier when she's here, because no man tries to chat me up. Do you want me to tell you why they behave so?"

"I know that no matter what I say, you will tell me. So go ahead."

" 'Cause them name man."

"What?"

" 'Cause he name man. Men can always do what they want and no one ever questions them."

"What are you saying?"

"That word 'man' carries a lot of weight in this world. It makes them believe they can do what they want and don't care if they hurt someone. I came to that conclusion long ago. That man who come in earlier, he liked what he saw and thought he could say what he wanted to me 'cause he name man. He doesn't stop to think I might have someone. But he name man and can do what he want. Your father, he behave bad and no one say anything. Not one person. And the only reason they all get away with it is 'cause them name man."

"Mammie, relax."

"You know, Kai, when Hayden hurt you, I felt it. I was young once, and back then you truly thought a man will bring you happiness. That's why you please and please them until you forget yourself. That was how I behaved with your father. I never once spoke about him to you. Whenever I think of him, even after all these years, my stomach still turns. But this wasn't fair to you. We're going to eat some cake, and I'll tell you a story about a man named Raphael Robbins."

CHAPTER EIGHT

Raphael Robbins

The door to the shop is closed. The room is dim. One light is on, its illumination not strong enough to fully brighten the room. The darkness doesn't bother us. A slice of cake cut earlier sits on my plate. The fork lies abandoned next to the dish. My mother has a story to tell and I need to hear every word.

"I remember when I first met your father, my body was ripe like a fruit ready to be picked. But in truth, I wasn't yet a woman, though I was no longer a child. It wasn't early in the morning, 'cause the sun was up high in the sky. But it was long before noon. I was at the market, buying fish to fry for lunch. There were people all about

the place, and I felt someone push against me. When I
turned around, that was when I saw him. What a smile he
had! That was the first thing I noticed about him—clean,
white, white, white teeth, like those perfect ones in the
movies. All I remember is that our eyes met. He didn't
even wait for me to say hi—he just walked right over like
he knew me for a long time. I didn't know what to do, but
as he got closer, the blood rushed so fast to my head that I
felt my heart go thump thump thump."

Raphael Robbins arrived in Antigua on a boat that
was making its way along the archipelago of islands in
the Lesser Antilles. Although he was born on this island,
his family moved away when he was a child, and he had
no memories of Antigua. When he finally stepped foot
on his birth place, he'd been travelling the Caribbean for
several months. Wherever he went, he always compared
that new place to his adopted homeland, Dominica. That
was why as soon as the sailors on the boat yelled, "Land,"
he hurriedly ran to the deck to see the island of his birth.
When he surveyed this new land mass, he quickly noted
how vastly different it was from Dominica. Here, the
land sloped into gentle hill after gentle hill. Although
it was beautiful, it was not the dramatic triumph of the
mountains he knew. The coastline was interesting, dotted
with an inordinate number of pristine white beaches that
created small, pretty coves. He recognized the familiar
foliage of the tropics, like the coconut and breadfruit
trees, but he quickly realized this place suffered from
drought and was not as bountiful as Dominica.

The life of a sailor did not agree with Raphael. He didn't enjoy being cooped up on a brig with sweaty men and desperately missed the feel of a woman. As the boat travelled the Caribbean, he discovered the many pleasures that could be bought in whorehouses and became very familiar with this type of transaction. In these dens of vice, Raphael explored the dark side of his nature. As soon as the boat docked, he'd gather his earnings and make his way to the local brothel.

When he arrived in Antigua, he had no desire to visit any relatives and kept to his regular itinerary as he put his money in his pants pocket, ready to invest in some pleasure. While he was disembarking, the captain, who knew that Raphael was no different than most of the other men who worked on the ship, warned him that he'd leave the following morning, whether he was on the boat or not, and jokingly added, "Don't fall asleep in the wrong bed, because I'm not waiting for you to wake up."

Raphael laughed and retorted, "Nothing will keep me. I haven't met a pussy so sweet yet."

He never knew why he chose Penelope other than the fact that she was the most attractive of the three remaining whores. After visiting so many of these establishments, Raphael went through a lengthy process to scrutinize the women to figure out who'd agree to his needs. As he followed Penelope to her room, he enjoyed looking at the sway of her voluptuous bottom but was also questioning his choice, because she was a little bit older than what he usually preferred. He didn't know if

she had a randy side to her nature, which he needed. This
hesitancy stayed with him up to the moment she closed
the door and they were alone in a room.

The small space had a large bed, and as she touched
its edge, she turned and asked him what he wanted. He
asked her to seductively undress for him. She was quiet
for a moment, and Raphael wondered if she was going to
barter for more money. Instead, she boldly caught his eyes
and began swinging her hips as she danced around the
cramped room. After she did that a few times, she somer-
saulted across the bed and landed in front of him, where
she sat and slowly unbuttoned her shirt. As it came off, he
saw she wore a black lace bra. Her breasts were bountiful,
appearing to be spilling out of her bra. She looked up
at him and shook them. His eyes were transfixed as
she unclasped her bra and they tumbled forth. Then
she walked over to him, stood in front of him, put his
hands on top of hers, and together they began caressing
her breasts. Moving away from him, she again used the
bed as a prop as she lay there, teasing him as her hands
slowly moved down her abdomen and stopped at her
zip. While she pretended to have problems with it, she
used her other hand to lift her skirt. As her hands started
to slide beneath her skirt, he felt himself getting harder
and harder. At that moment, he walked across the room,
slapped her across the face, tore off her panties, threw her
on the ground and mounted her.

She shifted slightly and looked up. Their eyes met,
and as he looked into them, they both lost themselves in

the moment, forgetting this was a monetary transaction. He became rougher, hitting her harder. To his surprise, she responded. As they scratched and bit each other they became like two animals. He knew her moans were real, not coaxed. Eventually, he felt her climax, and then he lost control and came. They lay there, breathless, silent, unsure what actually happened. The sounds from the adjoining rooms brought them to their reality, reminding them that they were inside a brothel. She smiled when he handed her the money, and then quietly invited him to her house for some off-the-clock adventure.

Day turned to night and then back to day again as the two of them got so entangled in their lust they forgot about time and Raphael experienced many free trips to her helm. When he awoke, it was daylight. Panicking when he saw the sun was up in the sky, he quickly bolted from her bed without saying goodbye.

By the time he reached the dock, the ship was chugging out of the harbour, heading to the horizon. He cursed loudly, but no one was around to hear. His lonely suitcase sat on the pier and he stood next to it while he watched the ship disappear from view. With no alternative, he picked up his suitcase, turned his back on the sea and made his way to the house of his only friend. She smiled when she saw him return. He put his mouth on hers, and they sealed their deal with a kiss. The two of them returned to bed, and that was how Raphael moved in with Penelope.

She never told him anything about her life. Penelope
was successful because she quickly realized that to
maintain a steady flow of clients, she needed to be more
than a sexual receptacle. She knew how to please a man
but also how to listen to his woes. They rewarded her
with large tips and regular visits. Her years of catering to
men gave her an insight into the human psyche. More
importantly, experience taught her that men spoke freely
on the pillow of a stranger. So she was not surprised
when Raphael confided that he was actually born in
Antigua but his family moved to Dominica when he was
a child. At night, he thought about this beloved island
and wanted desperately to return but feared he couldn't.
Penelope was used to confessions, and Raphael's was
no different.

His story was simple. He had a taste for young women
and had run from some trouble in Dominica. This girl
was much younger than him—a virgin, so she didn't know
another man's touch and believed the rough sex he liked
was how men and women made love. He confessed to
Penelope that the next woman he'd seek would also be
innocent, because it was much easier to mold
young women.

The girl in Dominica was the daughter of a very
prominent doctor, and her relationship with him, a poor
man, was her rebellion. At night, while her parents were
sleeping in their beds, she'd sneak out and meet him at
the river. There in the darkness of the night, they'd take
off their clothes and dive into the refreshing water. With

the cool water caressing their bodies, she'd wrap her legs
around him. He was always rough with her but carefully
bruised her in places where no one could see them. And
the next time they'd meet, he enjoyed feeling the swollen
skin that he'd hurt the night before.

One night, distraught, she confessed she was pregnant.
Those words silenced him. He saw her looking to him
for guidance but turned around and left her standing by
herself at the river. In his desperation, he didn't stop to
look back, so he didn't see her break down and cry when
she realized she had no one.

She couldn't hide her pregnancy. Her father slapped
her across the face. Then, he told her he'd get this man
to do the honourable thing as he pulled out his shotgun
from the cupboard. His best friend, the chief of police,
calmed him and arranged for Raphael's arrest. He assured
his friend the man would marry his young daughter. The
girl was fifteen. Raphael was thirty. He could choose jail
or marriage.

Raphael learned of this plan from his brother, a
policeman. He quickly packed a suitcase, desperately
hoping that there was a boat or a ship that he could sneak
on. A lonely vessel sat at the dock, and Raphael lied to
the captain about his seaworthiness. As he watched him
saunter onto the ship, the captain instinctively knew this
man had slept with the wrong woman.

Once they'd sailed safely out of the harbour, Raphael
laughed off the incident. He looked at the immense
span of water and realized that he was about to discover

the world. Raphael was not one for hard work and went hiding whenever summoned to duty. Not suffering Raphael's antics, the captain sent sailors to pull him from his hiding place. He told him that he better start earning his keep or he'd be thrown into the water and he could be certain that nobody would report it. Raphael wasn't sure if the captain was serious but knew he was capable of this act. So he started to work. Leaving Dominica, the ship headed south to Guyana and then turned around, working its way north along the archipelago of the Caribbean.

Penelope helped Raphael find work by asking a client to hire him in his shop and lied about his abilities. That was how Raphael found himself on the other side of a barber chair with a pair of scissors in his hand. He nicked heads and gave many bad haircuts before he became adept at his newfound trade. Over the next few months, he settled into life in Antigua. Eventually, he moved out of Penelope's home, but he still visited her very frequently. There were no tears between the two of them when he departed, because it was always understood that their living arrangement was temporary. However, their bodies still craved each other, and whenever she had downtime, he'd make his way over to her house.

It was there in Antigua that he heard the sounds of the Ancestors for the first time. He thought he was going crazy when their voices came into his head and tried to hush them by putting his hands over his ears and

screaming loudly, but it didn't work. Desperate to stop
their voices, he remembered his father saying that he'd
left Antigua because of these sounds. He wrote a letter to
his father to find out about the Ancestors, and his father
responded that he could not fight them, it was the family
legacy. For generations, one male from the family has
heard them. He told Raphael it was his cross to bear. The
Ancestors spoke, but he never allowed them to
infiltrate him.

Raphael first saw my mother at the market. Noticing
her youthful stance, he enjoyed watching her walk as
she twisted her waist from side to side, like a swirling
top. He remembered the young woman he'd shaped in
Dominica—his control of her. That same desire returned.
He thought: *She will be my next woman.* My mother
was oblivious to him as she interacted with vendors and
negotiated the price of the goods; she was neither forceful
nor pushy, which confirmed to him she'd be a good,
docile mate.

When he bumped into her, my mother was talking to a
fisherman. For a moment, everything was hushed. All she
could remember was him saying, "His fish isn't fresh like
he told you. I know someone whose fish is better." Then
this strange man with a different accent grabbed her hand
and before she could say anything pulled her away. With
his chocolate-brown skin glistening in the sun, she felt
the first stirring of her womanhood—everything around
her receded.

She was speechless when he asked how much fish
she needed. Instead, she handed him the money. Still no
words were said. In his lilting voice, my father told her his
name. My mother didn't reply, being aware how her hand
tingled as he held it.

"Standing there, I never knew anything about men,
so I really believed that he was great. I was so wrong. I
was easy to seduce because he sounded different than
everyone around me. The first thing I asked him was,
'Where are you from?' He told me, 'From Dominica.'
Then his face lit up as he spoke of the mists in the
mountains. When I was done with the market, he said he
wanted to see me later, and I said, yes, yes, yes. I ran home
and fried up the fish quick, quick for my brothers. Then
out I went to meet him."

He was nice at first. Her youthful world revolved
around him. One day she went to his house and took off
her clothes for him. After Raphael Robbins lay with my
mother, he grabbed her hand and told her she couldn't
leave. She thought he was playfully holding her and tried
to get him to release his hold, but his grip tightened and
he began to hurt her. As she tried to wriggle out of his
clasp, he told her that the more she moved, the harder it
would hurt. So she became quiet, and didn't notice that
he smiled when he released her black-and-blue wrist.
Horrified by the sight of her bruised wrist, she pulled
away from him. He apologized and said it wouldn't
happen again. In her youthful innocence, she
believed him.

The first time she experienced the true Raphael Robbins was around two weeks after they were living together. She arrived home in a happy, carefree mood, her basket filled with fresh food she'd just purchased—planning to prepare it for lunch. The vendors at the market had given her some deals. The day felt wonderful. When she breezily opened the door and saw him standing in the living room with a belt in his hand, her body instinctively froze. She couldn't move.

"Where were you?" he asked.

Tentatively, still not afraid, she showed him the food she was going to cook. "Look at what I have in the basket. It's full of some nice, nice, fresh food that I will make for you," she replied very carefully.

"You a lie! You were with another man," he yelled, lunging at her.

"No, I told you I was at the market. It's the truth. See, look at the basket . . ."

"You were gone too long to be at the market. You have some next man? Eh? Tell me. Are you spreading them sweet young legs for another man?"

"No," she cried—tears were coming to her eyes. "You the only man I ever let touch me. Me swear on the Bible."

"You lie. You're a whoring woman. I'm sure you done gone and give someone else that sweet pussy of yours." And then he took the belt and started hitting her. She ran into a corner, trying frantically to evade him. When she put up her hands to defend her face, he got more enraged. He dropped his belt, took his fist and hit her in the stomach over and over again. Then he dragged her to the bed, tore off her clothes and plied open her legs. After he came, he was still very excited and remained hard. He pulled her hair, slapped her once more and again forced himself inside of her. Her pleas to stop were met with a fist. After he was sexually satisfied, he fell asleep on top of her. She dared not move, afraid to wake him.

When he awoke, she was still lying beneath him, too scared to move. He got up and removed his flaccid manhood from inside her, acting as if nothing had happened. She went to the bathroom to clean the blood.

As he passed her in the bathroom, he threatened, "I'm warning you now, you can never tell no one about this or I'll kill you. And I never want to hear that you're with some next man again. I can never trust you, and that's why you can't go nowhere without me. From now on, I'm going to lock you in this house so you can't leave. I own you. Never forget that you belong to me."

Then he locked her in the bedroom. From that time forth, my mother only left the house when he was with her or if he gave permission. If he ever sent her on an errand, he timed her absence. If he thought she took too long, he always beat her and then had sex. The beatings were frequent—for little incidents: he did not like how she cooked the food; he thought there was dirt on the floor.

During that time, my mother also realized that he saw another woman. Not only could she smell her perfume on him, but he also told her about Penelope. A friend warned

her that he was a nasty man because he was often seen
at the home of a prostitute. She now knew the truth. He
stopped hiding his relationship with Penelope and often
told her that maybe she should go to this woman and get
training on how to please a man.

One Sunday morning, he surprised her by saying they
were going to the country. "To this day, I never knew why
he took me to Montula," my mother adds. "When I look
back, this is the only good memory I have of him."

In a chatty mood on the way there, he revealed that
he heard the voices of the Ancestors, and he added that
he never knew what to do with these voices that told
him stories from the past. That day, as he spoke of these
sounds that haunted him, she remembered the man she
first fell in love with. He told her to bend her head into
the wind, but she couldn't hear anything, and took her to
the burial place of the former slaves, where he repeated
the tales they told him. When he finished speaking, he
pulled her softly to him and my mother relaxed. He took
his time to learn about her body, and for the first time in
her life she climaxed. That was when I was conceived.

Before she realized it, my father knew my mother
was with child. When he saw her throw up the food she
cooked, he didn't beat her. He knew she wasn't wasting
his precious money, because her flat belly was beginning
to protrude.

"You with child," he said.

"What you mean? How did that happen?" she asked.

"Are you that fooly? Woman, there is a baby in your

belly. And it better belong to me, because when that child comes out, if it's not mine, I'm going beat you so bad that you might never walk again."

I was her first child, but Raphael was unsure how many other children he'd fathered. Raphael proclaimed the unborn child would be a boy and she believed him. By the time that I was conceived, my mother thought men controlled the world. Wherever she looked, she never saw a man who was afraid of saying what was on his mind, even if what he said was sheer stupidity. She thought money came easier for men (her brothers took a boat to sea and returned with fish to sell at the market; Raphael, adept with a pair of scissors, paid their rent)—she didn't know any woman having it that easy. Since she wanted the best for her child, she wished for a boy.

The night was still dark when I was born. The dawn had yet to come. When I emerged from her womb, she felt a momentary disappointment, hearing the midwife say, "It's a girl." Then I was put in her arms and she looked at me. In that moment, she realized that we were both women. With me in her arms, she was aware that she couldn't love a boy child as much as she loved me.

My father said, "How you make a girl when I told you that I only wanted a boy? It doesn't matter 'cause when she gets bigger, I'll have another person to bang."

He became an unhappier man, blaming everyone around him for his unhappiness: my mother, whom he still beat, and me, whom he rarely held. Hearing the voices of the Ancestors, he tried to drown them with alcohol. And as his hate for everything around him grew, he received a message from Dominica that his brother had died. Raphael blamed himself for his twin brother's death.

His twin was seriously injured in a motorcycle accident. Upon his unconscious arrival at the hospital, the staff immediately prepared him for surgery. As the chief surgeon entered the operating room, he looked at the face of the patient. He stared at the man for a long time, then removed his surgical gloves.

"I can't do this," he said and left the room.

This esteemed surgeon, the only man on the island with the skill to save his brother, was the father of the young girl Raphael got pregnant before fleeing Dominica. After this girl realized he was not coming back, she jumped over a cliff into the Caribbean Sea. When her father saw her lifeless body, he cried, and he never stopped crying.

With Raphael's twin lying on an operating table in need of his expertise, the doctor finally had the opportunity to take something from Raphael, like Raphael took his daughter from him. He told the hospital that he couldn't operate because this man's brother killed his daughter.

Raphael's brother died. In my father's grief he took long walks to the seashore, where he stared in the direction of Dominica. Some days his eyes deceived him, and he thought he saw the beautiful mists rise in the mountains. The sea became the flowing rivers that gave Dominica its lush vegetation and greenness. The sound of the waves breaking at the shore became the sound of the constant rainfall that gave his adopted homeland its dense foliage. There were times when his brother's face appeared before him, and he'd move his arms into the air to touch him—only to discover it was a mirage. He looked at the horizon, with the endless water sitting in front of him, and knew he was no longer in Dominica. This island had no majestic mountains that gave birth to a rich soil. And one morning, as he sat by the seaside, the thought of leaving Antigua came to him.

My father left the island before I turned one. He never heard me say, "Daddy"; he never saw me take my first steps, and he never knew the joy of feeling my hand in his as we walked down the road.

One night, he returned home and told my mother he was going away and not coming back.

"What you say? I'm not sure that I heard right," my mother replied in disbelief.

"You heard me. I'm leaving you and this pickney. And me not coming back."

Then he took the same old worn-out suitcase that the captain left on the pier several years back and packed his clothes.

"You can't do this. I love you."

"I'm free to do what me want. I don't answer to no one, especially not a woman."

"Raphael, what 'bout Kai? She's your pickney." As she spoke, he turned and hit her.

"Shut up, woman. I'm tired of hearing you speak. That child is your child. I never wanted her, but she came and I can't send her back."

"Don't go. Please don't leave me," she pleaded.

"Woman, I can do what I please." And he turned around and hit her again. She felt dizzy, then she touched the blood oozing down the side of her mouth. He looked at her and laughed.

"If I keep banging you up like this, your face will get so twisted up no other man will want you."

He continued filling the suitcase. My mother then wrapped her arms around his legs and begged him to stay. He ignored her. She held onto him as he walked around the room to get his things. He enjoyed dragging her— scrapping her skin. When his suitcase was packed, he kicked her so hard she released her hold and he made his way to the door.

She ran after him. As he walked away, he noticed her walking behind him and paused to tell her the truths about his life that he'd kept hidden. He told her about the girl who jumped into the Caribbean Sea. He told her that if she was so upset, then she and her child could join this woman, sharing the same fate. Then, when he finished speaking, he attempted to swing at her one last time. His hands met air. He looked around and saw she was no longer following him, but was standing far away, watching. This further angered him, and he furiously ran back to start hitting her. He swung his arm to the left; he swung it to the right and he kept going. When he realized she was not moving, he stopped, turned around and calmly walked back to his suitcase. Hoisting it onto his shoulder, he never looked back.

When consciousness returned, my mother felt as if her body had been hit by a car. She somehow dragged herself back to the house. Not attempting to clean the blood that was now caked onto her face and her body, she felt so bruised that she collapsed onto the bed, thinking this was a dream and when she awoke, her world would be the same.

My wails woke her. She turned on the bed, saw her stained blood on the sheets and realized that it was real. She screamed.

It was Vee, her neighbour, who came to her. She had often heard my father beating my mother. The sight of my mother's pulverized body really upset her, but she remained calm, not wanting my mother to realize the extent of her injuries. Vee wrapped her in sheets, cradled me in her arms and took us to the doctor.

The doctor was shocked. He whispered to Vee that there should be a law that would put my father in jail for a long, long time as he gently and carefully bandaged my mother's cracked ribs and wounds. He prescribed a lot of rest. That day, Vee moved into our house and tended to my mother and me.

My father was last seen standing on the deck of a ship docked at the harbour, about to sail to exotic places. A man he knew saw him and called, but Raphael pretended not to hear. He stood on that deck, and as the ship sailed out of the harbour, he watched the island disappear—each hour distancing him, erasing the memory of the woman and child he left behind.

In her despair my mother didn't respond to anything or anyone. She lay in bed, staring at the ceiling. Vee's attempts to get her interested in life fell short. She was as if comatose.

When one day Vee was called away for an emergency—forced to leave my mother and me alone—with no one around I crawled next to her and smothered her bruised face with soft, sweet kisses. Feeling my innocent lips on her skin, my mother stirred. She wrapped her arms around me, looking into my eyes. Her bruised face stared back at her and she started to cry. I put my small arms around her. Though her hands were cut and pained her, she pulled me close to her and said, "I will begin again, Kai. We woman. We never quit."

After she told me the story, we were silent. Then my mother confided, "I'm not going to lie to you, but there was a time when I wanted Raphael to return. It's sad but true that when a woman is hit for so long, she believes this is how things go. Up to this day, I often wonder what would have happen to us if Vee wasn't around.

"Kai, when you're young, you do too much and give too much 'cause you believe man is god. I've come to understand that it's not really about love or giving.

"I never knew what happened to Raphael. Kai, it pains

me to say this, but your father enjoyed hurting people. He was a bad man. Even now, when I think about him, I can't think of anything good. People always wonder how I could live with a man and then find myself with a woman. I can't answer that question. All I know is that I can love. People say that love has all these twists and turns, but I don't think so. Life is simple if you really look at it. Vee was good to me and that taught me love."

I never knew if my mother came to Vee as a rebound love or if she discovered love through her. I don't think it mattered to either of them. But the writer in me wondered if their stories would have overlapped if Raphael Robbins never entered my mother's life.

CHAPTER NINE

Prelude To A Beginning

My mother is busily beating butter and sugar, preparing a cake to celebrate Vee's return from St. Lucia, when Vee calmly announces, "It's time we build a new home for us to live in."

The hum of the small electric mixer muffles her words. My mother thinks she heard "build a new home" but isn't sure. Because she didn't catch every word, she promptly turns off the mixer, giving Vee her full attention.

"What you say?" she asks.

Vee calmly replies, "It's time we build a home for us."

This time the words are clear; my mother hears every syllable. My mother looks at her partner of over twenty years and says, "Vee, you mad or something? You can't drink water before you reach pond. I know and you know that we don't have enough money in the bank to build a house."

"That's what you think," Vee adds with a mischievous twinkle in her eye as she hands her a printout of their recent bank statement. My mother inspects the paper, and her mouth opens wide with shock at the balance.

She turns to Vee in astonishment. "Is this a joke? Did the bank mix up our account with someone else? I know we don't have this kinda money."

"Yes, we do."

"How we come by it?"

There is a playful glint in Vee's eyes as she calmly explains, "I inherited it."

"What you mean?" my mother replies with her mouth wide open.

"My father left me all this money."

Speechless, my stunned mother sits down and stares; she looks again at the bank book before she speaks. "That's shocking. How he get this kinda money? And why he give you 'cause that man forget about you all these years."

"When they read the will, I kept saying, 'This isn't true,' but the lawyer confirmed it: this money belongs to me."

"You mean this is no joke? You serious?"

"Yes, this money belongs to us. It was so hard for me to hold my tongue while I was gone. I was dying to tell you. But I decided to hold off 'cause I wanted to see your expression," Vee replies, affectionately wrapping her arm around my mother.

"Woman, you nearly give me a heart attack when I saw the balance. What you think get into his head? Why he leave you all this money?"

"I don't know, but my eldest brother told me that just before he died, he changed the will."

My mother chuckles. "Vee, it's his insurance. He did this 'cause he's afraid of going to hell for his bad deed. He's finally looking God in His face for the first time. He can't tell Him that he throw him sixteen-year-old daughter out the house without a cent to her name."

As they chuckle, Vee adds, "You right, my love. As a child, all he ever speak 'bout is living happily in the hereafter." Then in a more serious voice, Vee changes the subject, "It's time we own a house. With the money we saved and what he left me, let's buy a plot of land big enough to build two houses: one for us and one for Kai. She's a big woman now and doesn't need to be under our roof, but it'd be nice to have her next door."

"I like that and I can't wait to tell Kai the good news." My mother relaxes into Vee's arms.

I arrive home well after midnight and expect the house to be in darkness, but to my surprise, my mother and Vee are sitting in the living room, quietly sipping tea, waiting for me. I assume they are up because Vee just returned from St. Lucia earlier that day and wanted to tell me about her trip.

As I hug Vee, I ask, "How was St. Lucia?"

"Kai, the last time I saw my father he was wearing a hat as he said his final words to me, 'I don't want no funny child. People will think I'm not a man of God because I made a child like you.' He was a tall man with this air of importance, but when I saw him lying in the coffin, I realized he was not as big as I thought. You know, until he was on his deathbed, he never even told my brothers how to get in touch with me."

My mother sucks her teeth and mutters, "He only saying this 'cause he feeling Satan's fork digging him bottom."

Vee and I smile, but we ignore her as I continue, "This is so sad because you lost all these years with your brothers. What did you tell them when they asked what you've been up to all these years?"

"I looked them in the eye and told them, 'I don't have a man. I have a woman. We live under the same roof and sleep in the same bed.'"

"Did that shock them?"

"No. My father confessed that I shamed him. Looking back, I don't think any of this surprised them, because ever since I was a little girl, everyone used to say that I wasn't right."

"People always a talk," my mother interjects.

"Shush and let me finish my story. Sometimes you need to be quiet," Vee says as she warmly nudges my mother. "One day, we'll go to St. Lucia and meet my family. I told them about our shop and they were proud."

Before my mother interrupts, I answer, "It's good to have you back. I know Mammie really missed you. The house wasn't the same without you."

"Speaking of houses, we need to move."

"Why? Is there a problem?" I look at my mother, imploring her to speak, but her expression is unreadable.

Vee's face is different. Her eyes glisten with excitement, and when she answers, her voice is highly animated. "We can live here, but we don't need to. My father left me some money and we're going to build two homes, one for you and one for us."

"You serious?" I ask in total surprise.

The two of them nod their heads in unison and Vee tells me about her inheritance.

After she finishes, I reply, "I'm speechless. I really don't know what to say. How come he left you the money? I thought he didn't approve of you."

My mother answers, "He 'fraid hell more than anything else."

Vee adds, "I think this money gave my father a place in heaven."

I close my eyes, digesting this information, and the Ancestors tell me it's time I join them at Montula. I quickly glance at my mother and Vee, wondering if possibly now they also heard them, but I quickly realize they didn't.

I've only known this house, and I tell my mother and
Vee that I want to carry some of the wood planks on the
floor to our new home because they carry the imprint
of my first baby steps and my conversations with the
Ancestors. Under this roof, I discovered how to hold
a pen and then fill a blank paper with words. And it is
inside these walls I learned about the joy of a man's touch
and the intense pain he causes when his hands no longer
caress your skin.

They smile, and then my mother reveals her thoughts.
"When I was growing up, my mother sat me down and
looked me straight in the eye and said, 'Woman own
nothing without a man, so go find one.' Back then, she
was right; man seem to own everything. Things different
today, as woman good for themselves and they do what
they need to do to get by. I know when my mother saw
me with Kai's father, she thought I did well 'cause he was
older, and she thought he'd settle down with me. After he
left, even though she saw he banged me up, she told me
go find another man 'cause I will need one to take care of
me and Kai. That was when I stopped listening to her."

Vee adds, "All I ever heard come from my father's
mouth is that woman come from Adam's ribs. Up to this
day, I can recall his big booming, preacher voice telling
me that a woman must be obedient to a man." Vee stands
up and begins imitating her dad, dropping her voice a few
octaves: "'God gave man dominion over all things and
that includes woman,' he often said. One of his favourite
pieces of scripture was from the New Testament. His

thundering voice shouted, 'In First Corinthians, chapter eleven, verse three, the Lord said, *But I would have you know, that the head of every man is Christ; and the head of the woman the man.* Our Lord implicitly states a woman needs a man. I am the man of the house, and I will teach you to be servile and obedient. You will be a good woman.'"

My mother rolls her eyes. "Pure rubbish."

Vee smiles in agreement.

My mother, Vee and I arrive at Montula under a blue, blue sky. Nearly twenty years have passed since my mother, taking my small childish hand, guided me on this forgotten road. Little about this desolate spot filled with overgrown trees and alive with wild bush, butterflies and birds has changed. Here the mahogany trees' lush growth creates a canopy of green over the roadway to shield the earth from the sun. I love its wild state and deep, penetrating silence. This is where the sweet, soft breeze sings the melodies of the Ancestors in their purest form.

As we make our way along the road, the sweet songs of the birds caress the air, while the cool breeze kisses our cheeks. Because anyone who learns that this was once a graveyard for slaves doesn't want to live here, there is no settlement in this area. There are rumours that one can see a dead man walk at night and the ghosts howl even when there is no moon. Although there are no markers and no one knows where the bodies lie, people avoid this old graveyard.

I lead them to a spot where there is an old, rotting sign: LAND FOR SALE. The three of us are still as we take in the quiet, the view and the solitude. Standing under one of the large trees, we look at the wide expanse of land where the green hills gracefully slope downward until they touch the sea. The quiet invades me. I close my eyes.

Vee breaks the reverie. She asks in a hushed voice, as if fearing to break the quiet, "where is this place?"

"It's Montula," my mother whispers, as if not wanting to wake the Ancestors.

"How come I've never heard about it?"

"They used to bury slaves here and people say the place full of jumbies. That's why no one wants to come here."

"I like that. I really, really, really like that. Then we don't have to deal with people. The silence so nice and I know I will enjoy the quiet. I think the best part about this place is that there are no neighbours and we don't have to tell them to mind their business," Vee announces. Her voice is sure. "I think this is where we should live. What's going on in your heads? Are you scared about living on an old gravesite?"

"If this is where our people are buried, they won't hurt us. We didn't put them in no early grave. They know how much we have to fight to survive. I believe their spirits are our friends," my mother replies.

That afternoon, with the sun high in the sky and a peaceful silence surrounding us, my mother, Vee and I decide that we will build our new homes at Montula with our ancestors.

Two homes are built on the hill: one for my mother and Vee and another for me. Neither house is the same, because we have different needs. But both homes have something that we never had before: large, airy rooms. I incorporate many special features and design options that Hayden drew many years ago, when we were teenagers. I finally have a special writing room replete with a balcony, where I spend days and nights, writing and speaking with the Ancestors. It is in this room, situated at Montula, where the Ancestors speak so clearly, I write my greatest works.

The years pass and we find great happiness in this spot. My life changes drastically when my short story book is published and then I write a novel. Also discovering I can write plays, I create scripts that are performed on stage.

There was a time when I only knew the shores of this island, but my success takes me across the Caribbean and to other lands. I am the embodiment of the Ancestors' dreams—a writer and a playwright—finally their stories are no longer lost in the wind.

With my life blossoming, I learn that love has many forms when a new man enters my life. Duane makes me rediscover my heart. We meet while I'm overseeing the production of one of my plays. After a day of hard work and rehearsals, the crew decides we need a break and suggests an outing at a popular night spot for some live music, where someone claims, "The best singer in the Caribbean serenades the crowd."

That is how I find myself sitting on a stool, coolly sipping a drink, waiting for the evening entertainment to begin. While there, I hear spontaneous laughter coming from the corner and turn to look. A tall, well-built man with a goatee is standing amongst a group of strangers. As he delivers another quick retort, he looks up. Our eyes connect—in that nanosecond, I unexpectedly feel a jolt. He nods; I smile back. He quickly excuses himself from his group and makes his way over, easily occupying the empty seat next to me.

"Hello, lovely lady," he says, "I haven't seen you before."

"That's because I've never been here," I calmly reply. With him standing so close to me, I'm now wholly conscious of his strong sexual aura.

"Hmmm, a newbie. I guess you're from a foreign?" He asks.

"No. I'm a born and bred Antiguan."

"If you're Antiguan, why haven't we met?" He looks me directly in the eye, "I'd remember seeing a pretty face like yours."

"Sometimes I get so caught up in my life that I forget to take downtime."

"I'm glad that you made it tonight." His eyes look deep into mine. "I felt drawn to you and that's why I came over—it's like we're star-crossed lovers, Romeo and Juliette."

"But I want a better outcome. Drinking poison isn't my thing," I reply as he laughs.

"What brings you out tonight?"

"I love live music and my friends suggest it's a good place to unwind."

He smiles as he sings his response. "The music here is exceptional."

"My friends told me the singer has the best voice on the island."

"He is legendary. And the girls love him. You might need to watch yourself— you could fall for him."

"Maybe it'll be the reverse, he'll jump off the stage to be with me."

"You'd be worth it." Flirtatiously, he smiles at me.

"Who are you? You seem to know a lot about this singer?" I ask.

"I live for my music. Some people come here for escape, others for enjoyment. I know you want to see the entertainment. Tell me about you? What's your passion?"

"My writing."

"What do you write? Are you a journalist?" His eyes appear to pierce me. He quietly replies, "No, you're too artsy. I can see you writing a steamy novel about two star-crossed lovers who meet on stools."

"Yes, I'm a storyteller but I'm not too sure about that plot . . . we may need to—"

He interrupts, "Now I know why you're so familiar. You're Kai Robbins. I've seen your picture in the newspaper. Hmmm, you're so much prettier in life." Then he adds, "I'd make a great character for a story."

"Why? What's so interesting about you?"

He leans into me as he whispers in my ear, "I'm going

to make you so much happier. By the way, my name is
Duane. As much as I'm enjoying talking with you, I've got
to go, but I promise I'll be back. Pretty lady, please keep
this seat warm for me."

I smile as he leaves. The lights dim; the music begins.
A voice as sweet as sugar cake and as bright as its dye
floats in the air. I close my eyes, absorbing his sugary
sound; then I open them and look at the stage. His
globular eyes catch mine and we exchange a smile. The
singer with the smooth voice was the man who sat next to
me on the stool.

When the show is over, he comes over to me and
we laugh. The nightclub empties, but we are still there.
We stay at that bar with the mosquitoes buzzing but
not biting; high in the sky the stars twinkle. The night
turns into dawn and we're still talking, his creative spirit
melding with mine. I've spent so many years on my own,
with no one to share my thoughts, that I welcome Duane.
I quickly discard the loneliness of my life, as he under-
stands my imagination. It's so easy to be with him. Our
thoughts align.

Duane's skin is as dark as mine and his hair as tightly
curled, but there our physical similarities end. His large
eyes appear like round circles in his face. His physique is
perfectly slim and muscular after years of performing.

On the following day, I return to the venue. The room
is packed, but our eyes find each other, and he smiles
brightly. When he finishes performing, he crosses the
room with quick strides and surprises me when his full

lips find mine and claim me. Like the hands of the clock that moves forward, our hearts bond. We can't stop what is happening.

Duane and I leave and walk along the beach. The waves lap. The moon is a small sliver in the sky and the millions of stars twinkle. One can live in the Caribbean her entire life, but there are moments when its magnificent beauty leaves you breathless. When that mood takes hold, you delve past the borders of your existence like we do this night. Our bodies have not discovered the joy of intimacy, when my dormant heart begins beating from the sound of his melodious voice. Its strong thump shocks me; its reactivation momentarily paralyzes me. As I look into his round eyes, I instinctively know I was meant to be with him.

Again, we speak until the moon disappears; then I take him to my home at Montula, where he pulls me to him. In a moment of contentment, he slips easily into me. That night, I feel a willingness to step outside my skin and experience something new.

We are as natural as the coconut on the tree. At night I read my stories, and he raptly listens. One evening, he surprises me by saying, "I wrote a new song. Do you want to hear it?"

I nod enthusiastically.

"I know this might sound crazy, but the words came to me when I was standing at your balcony. It's like a wind blew them at me. I quickly grabbed a pen and wrote this song and couldn't believe what I produced."

I smile as he speaks. I say nothing. Duane strums his guitar—his voice, sweetly fills the air and drifts into the breeze that blows stories—the Ancestors also hear his song.

With my songs so sweet and nice

I know my forefathers are enticed

To them I have one question to ask

Do you want to come back and play 'mas?

"Who care 'bout a jam," they say

"When there is so much in your way

Strong and mighty, we once cried

Young and proud, we died."

Their words are a large mystery

I feel they are commenting on history

I ask, "Tell me what you think about today?"

"Not much different than yesterday"

Astonished I look around town

Their words rock the ground . . .

Fancy car and pretty store

But your new lives close a door

You believe lies from a mouth that believe

he is right, but he is simply a thief

To you, he is the man wearing the suit

but he is only thinking about his loot

Promising gold, money and job . . .

But it's we, he continues to rob

Words and promise is all he say

We must realize it, my brother, today

In the past, it was the slavemaster

Now all we hear is politician laughter

We are always together. At night, our bodies urgently seek each other, and then he lies next to me and sings me love songs with such poignant honesty that I cry. I never question him or me or us. Through him, I come to understand that love has no ending, it is as infinite as the breeze that blows.

As my love life blossoms, Brittany calls me. "Kai, please come over. I have to see you urgently."

Brittany is still my best friend, and on the phone I detect something different in her voice. I panic because she doesn't sound like herself. She's just returned from a trip abroad to see her boyfriend and I hope everything went well. I instinctively go to her. My worries are quickly resolved when she opens the front door and flashes her left hand. The sun captures the large diamond ring.

We dance around the room in a celebratory fashion for several minutes before we contain ourselves. "Congratulations!" I scream.

I gush over the diamond, carefully inspecting it as she dreamily explains her Canadian boyfriend proposed. It's thrilling to see her beam with happiness after her earlier heartaches with Shaun.

"This is so much to take in," I say, "I can't believe that you're getting married. That means you're leaving the island."

Brittany confides, "I was really surprised by Brad's proposal! I didn't think we'd get married so quickly, but he told me he didn't want to waste any more time apart. He was tired of this long-distance relationship."

"I know this sounds selfish, but I don't know what I'll do when you're gone."

"Kai, now that you're a celebrated author, you're always travelling so you'll have to make regular stopovers to see me."

"Why can't he move here?"

"Kai, he's not from Antigua and has no intention of living here."

We are sitting on the porch of her house where her maid is serving us lunch.

"Brittany, you lived most of your life like a pampered doll, with your maid cooking and cleaning. How are you going to survive without a helper?"

"I'll have to learn. Kai, you are the closest person to me. You've always known I've dreamed of living in a city, surrounded by tall buildings, lights and lots of people. Now I will."

"I'm happy but I'll miss you."

"Let's not think about that. I want to talk about the wedding. You know, you're going to be my maid of honour."

"If you told me it was someone else, I'd be very upset."

"Good, that's settled. Prepare yourself because I'm getting married in three months. So the next little while is all about me. Hopefully, Duane won't mind me stealing so much of your time."

I smile mischievously. "Well, I may need to run home and get a taste of him every now and then—he's just so delicious."

With three months to plan Brittany's wedding, I'm thrust into her life, and it feels like we're in school again, as I spend most of my evenings and weekends with her. Every Saturday afternoon, we sit on the floor of her bedroom and giggle, like when we were teenagers. One afternoon, in the midst of our girlish laughter, her mother knocks on the door. As she stands on the threshold, talking about the wedding details, I stop listening—transported to my teenage years—remembering my uncontrollable excitement when Hayden used to visit. I quietly smile to myself. It's been a long time since I allowed myself to think about him.

After her mom leaves the room, Brittany notices a shift in my mood. "What's up? You don't seem like yourself."

"This may sound odd, but when your mom rapped on the door, for some strange reason, I was transported back to Hayden."

"Do you mean that handsome man who is my cousin?"

"None other."

"I still think the two of you were lucky to have found such a special love while you were so young. Some people never experience that in a lifetime."

"I won't argue with you on that. But I have Duane now."

"Yes, you do, and I like him very much. He allows your

artistry to flow." She switches the topic. "Did I tell you that Hayden's coming home for the wedding?"

I answer calmly, "I thought he would."

"Don't try and pretend that you're not curious to see him. I know you very well. You have to be. Don't you ever wonder if there is still something there? I do. Maybe it's the romantic in me that hopes my wedding will bring you two back together. You know what we say, 'Old fire tek easy fi ketch.'" (Old loves are easily ignited.)

I laugh. "He and I are an old-time story."

Her expression changes. "You may have been young, but I spent a lot of time with the two of you. The only thing I can say is you two flowed naturally. You were very similar. I may not know a whole lot about life, but this much I do: not many people get a chance to love the way you and Hayden did."

"Let's not talk about this. Hayden is the past. We haven't seen each other in years, and other than your updates, I have no idea what's going on in his life. Most of all, it doesn't matter anymore, because I have someone else in my life."

"Kai, I've been your best friend and seen you with both men. I like Duane a lot, and if you'd never loved Hayden the way you did, I'd think Duane was for you. Maybe my wedding might bring you and Hayden back to each other. I can probably swear on the Bible, even though I've never asked him, but I'm sure Hayden has read every word you've written."

"Brittany, enough. We don't need to speak about

Hayden anymore. I don't talk about your relationship with Shaun."

"You're right. But Shaun and I were different because we didn't fit together. I don't mean to speak ill of him, but Shaun wasn't a really nice person in those days. Maybe he's grown up. I don't care anymore. Looking back, I just wanted a boyfriend because that's what you want at that age. We didn't have very much in common. Sometimes things don't work because you're not right for each other. Let's forget about all of this old-time talk, I've got a wedding to plan."

Three days before the wedding, I'm at Brittany's house when the phone rings. As she's far from the phone, she yells at me to answer it.

I cheerfully answer, "Hello."

There's silence on the other end. I repeat myself. "Hello."

And then I hear him speak as he clears his throat. "Hi Kai, it's Hayden. How are you? You sound the same. I can't remember the last time we spoke."

I freeze. The truth is I'd know his voice even if I was standing in a crowd in a foreign country and he whispered my name. He continues, "Hey, Kai, are you there?"

Before I can respond, Brittany grabs the phone. "I know it's for me," she says as she gleefully takes the receiver.

She quickly realizes it's Hayden, looks over at me and mouths, "Sorry."

As I stare at the wall, his voice ringing in my ear, I overhear her say, "Yes, I'm excited. In a few days, I'll be a married woman."

There is silence and then she resumes speaking: "Yes, you can bring her. I'll see you at the wedding."

Announcing that Hayden will be coming to the wedding with someone we both knew from school, a very disappointed Brittany hangs up the phone.

"I never really liked her, but I couldn't tell him no," she explains. "I wonder how they met. Why should I ask? Hayden always has a girl in the wings, so I guess it shouldn't surprise me." She is thoughtful for a while before looking at me, her eyes intently piercing me. "I wanted to see if you two still have some spark. I think I'm right. I saw how you reacted, and I can assure you he was disappointed when he heard my voice."

I never reply.

A few days later, I cry when I assist Brittany into her wedding dress on the morning she takes her vows. My tears don't end there. They stream down my face when she walks down the aisle of a quaint church in the countryside as she smiles into the eyes of a man who isn't born of this soil; a man who will never understand why our Ancestors sing in the wind. It is a beautiful ceremony as the sweet Antiguan breeze keeps the church cool and the melodious moaning of the organ plays songs of love.

The reception is at a plush hotel. From the corner of his eyes Hayden sees me and smiles, but doesn't come over when he realizes Duane is at my side. Shortly after the reception begins, Brittany pulls me aside, gives me the key to her hotel room and asks me to meet her there since she needs to adjust her dress and makeup.

She isn't in the room, and I sit on the bed, knowing it might be a while because it won't be as easy for her to get away.

"Well, Kai, it's been seven years since we've been together in a room. I never thought that would ever happen again." Hayden's voice is shaky. We stare at each other, neither saying anything. I want to ask him if he was following me, but don't. He looks the same; nothing about him has changed; oddly, nothing felt uncomfortable about our closeness.

My calm voice surprises me when I finally speak. "Yes, Hayden, it's really nice to see you. How are you?"

He smiles, "Right now, all I can think is that you're still so beautiful. The truth is you look better—I never thought that was possible."

He hesitates for a moment; then he sits on the bed. I feel the thread that was once there still tugging. "A part of me wants to ask, 'How's life?' But I already know some of the answers. All your dreams came true. You're a writer. You've published books. People outside Antigua know your name. It doesn't surprise me. I always knew you'd do the impossible."

"Thanks, that means a lot. I've heard you've done well too. You're now working as an architect."

"I can't complain. But being honest, I didn't get everything I wanted."

He moves closer to me—his thigh rubbing against mine. "Do you ever think about what would have happened if you never overheard me?"

Hayden's eyes are penetratingly looking directly at me; a breeze blows into the room, seeming to push me closer to him.

"Hayden, I don't. This is what I think: if I didn't overhear you then, it would have come out in another way."

"I was a young man who did stupid things. Not only did I take you for granted, I abused your trust. I'm sorry because I never meant to hurt you."

"Life didn't end, although for a moment I felt like it did."

"Can I see you before I leave? I'd like to spend some time with you. There's more that I have to say."

"Are you serious?"

"Yes, I'd like to see you again. Is that such a strange request?"

'Hayden, I'm seeing someone. He wouldn't like it."

"Kai, this has nothing to do with him. This is me, Hayden. We shared many firsts. I'm asking to see you because I don't believe we've written the ending to us. I felt a pull from the moment I saw you, and it's not just because you look so beautiful. Please come up to my house. I just want to spend some time with you."

Brittany breezes into the room. She is so happy that she's oblivious to what's going on, and it doesn't register that Hayden and I are alone.

"Hayden, you know I love you, but I need to freshen up. So you've got to go. Kai is my maid of honour, and she's here to keep me glowing today."

"My beautiful cousin, I don't think you need her, because you're on top of the world."

"I am. I am. Everything is perfect. Now shoo."

She pushes Hayden out of the room. As I fix her makeup, she talks effusively about the wedding. Suddenly she is quiet. When she speaks again, she's much more serious. "I'm right."

"What are you talking about?"

"You and Hayden."

"Mind your business or I'll plaster this lipstick all over your face."

She giggles. "I won't say anything else, because I can't afford to look like a crazy woman on my wedding day."

When I return to the reception, Duane's strong hand holds mine. I feel comforted with him next to me. From the other side of the room, I see Hayden watching us, but he doesn't come over. After the wedding, I'm torn. It's not that I don't love Duane, but a part of me wants to see Hayden. I think about driving up that hill to see him, but I don't.

A few months after Brittany's wedding, I'm surprised when Duane tells me he's been offered a two-year singing contract in New York.

"Are you taking it?"

He nods.

"Why do you have to leave?" I ask, inside I'm screaming 'Why? Why? Why is this happening again?'

"I want to explore my opportunities."

"What does this mean for us?"

His eyes don't look at me. "Kai, I don't know. I can't make any promises. I know how I feel about you, but this is such a big break in my career."

A breeze blows. I know it's the Ancestors caressing me, telling me it will work out. The inhabitants of this island are used to the coming and going of its people, and that was why I was able to accept Duane's departure. I wasn't sure if he'd return but couldn't stop him.

Once Duane leaves, I ask my mother and Vee, "Can I build a statue in the yard?"

Puzzled by my request, they speak in unison. "Why?"

"We're living in a forgotten graveyard. Let's honour the dead. The voices that once lived are crying to be heard. We need a monument that commemorates our Ancestors. It will tell the story of their lives. This statue will remind us that we shouldn't forget them."

Vee nods and my mother replies, "Kai, I like that. I really like that a lot. Those politicians should have done something like this long ago with some of the money they thief."

On a gigantic steel sheet, shaped like a coffin, a
sculptor hammers impressions of the faces of boys, girls,
women, men. They are old; they are young. Some have
tentative smiles; others are mournful. When I first see it,
I momentarily look at it in total awe. My mother and Vee
are speechless. The sun's rays allow each face to glisten.
For the first few days after it's installed in the yard, the
three of us spend hours standing in front of the statue,
imagining the days and nights of the people mythicized
on it.

Word spreads around the island. We never expected
the statue at Montula would cause a stir, but people want
to see it. At first, there's the occasional car, but soon more
cars come. We grow used to hearing them drive up our
desolate road and seeing strangers stand in front of our
house, some venturing into the yard, standing before the
statue, where they pay homage to our Ancestors.

Although we now have visitors, the hill is still a
lonely spot. We love our solitary existence far from the
happenings on the island, in a place so many feared.
Some evenings, I smell the scent of my mother's and Vee's
baking as it wafts through the air. On those occasions
I often make my way to their home to eat. I often hear
their laughter. They love music, and I watch them dance
to the sounds of the Caribbean on their balcony. The hill
comes to life with our hum.

I love, early in the morning, stepping onto my balcony
to listen to the birds and watch them as they flutter
amongst the flowers. My writing flows as easily as the

rain falls from the sky—sometimes in light showers that sprinkle the earth, and at other times the Ancestors' words are like a torrential, furious downpour.

At night, I look up at the stars and hear their voices, drifting so clearly in the breeze. I am alone on my bed, feeling this sense of loneliness as I wonder if I'll ever find a man to love me who is rooted to this island. The Ancestors sense my restlessness, and one night when I stand in front of the statue, they recount the long-forgotten story of Montula.

CHAPTER TEN

The Story Of Montula

Wilfred received ten painful lashes when he tried to run away from the overseer who snarled, "You a man now. Time to work in the field." He remembered straining his head to look up at him and then glancing at the men preparing to go to the field. As there was a vast difference in height between him and all these men, he couldn't understand why the overseer told him he was now a man. It was plainly obvious he had several feet to grow.

At only six years old, Wilfred screamed when he felt the sting of the whip cutting into his skin, creating a red opening that left a permanent scar.

"Me still little," he whimpered to Old Meg as she applied a poultice to soothe his back. "Me only half the size of the men who work the land. Why they need me to go work in the field?"

Her voice was hollow. "It the way things are. Nah cry, boy. Do what them ask, and no one go hurt you."

Then she pulled a rag from her bosom, wiping the tears from Wilfred's young face. Her hollow brown eyes belied nothing, because she'd stopped crying many years ago. It took Wilfred awhile before he realized he couldn't hide from the overseer or from working in the field, but by then his back was tattooed with welts that resembled a turtle. Even in the field, he had to be careful because the overseer seemed to enjoy flicking his whip.

After one really bad lashing, he told Old Meg, "It not right how that man bang me."

"You not the only one. He treat we like we is an animal"—her voice remained hollow. Her withered fingers traced his scars. "Dat's why all our backs look like some animal."

"Before me die, me go make sure me hold me free paper in me hand," Wilfred said. "Then no man can whip me."

Old Meg looked around to make sure they were alone, and for the first time Wilfred heard emotions in her voice. "You have to be smarter than dem. Obey everything them say and them believe you tamed. Then massa go give you a plot to grow your food. It okay to let your belly grumble, 'cause you can sell some of the food you grow. Don't be

foolish with your money—save every penny. Dat the only
way you can buy your free paper."

Wilfred's limbs grew. His shoulders broadened—
muscles formed on his body—and he became a man.
His smooth dark skin and muscular body are the same as
those of the other ten male slaves on Nibbs's plantation,
but each man bears a different animal tattoo on his back.
Always before sunup, he tends to his plot before being
forced to go to work in Massa's field. Whenever he looks
up at the blue sky, he doesn't see its endless wonder.
Although he is only twenty, his eyes are already dull like
Old Meg's. Yet, at night, he dreams of his hand firmly
holding a piece of paper that'd allow him to walk freely,
without fear of the whip; these dreams are the unvoiced
words of his only hope.

Tula came to the plantation with smooth brown skin
and full, pouty lips shaped like a heart. Her skin wasn't
filled with welts like Wilfred's, but the lizard tattoo on
her back spoke of pain. Since her skin was a lighter shade
than most of the other slaves, everyone on the plantation
thought she was destined for a few weeks in Old Massa
Nibbs's bed, but he was so enthralled with Betsy that Tula
was sent to work in the fields. Each morning, she tied her
head and spoke with the other three women who worked
in the fields. Whenever one of the lustful men tried to
catch her attention, Wilfred saw the terror in her eyes.

It took several months before she stopped shaking
when he told her good morning. On the day that the rain

and wind were so powerful the slaves had to stay inside,
her brown eyes found his. From the moment Tula's and
Wilfred's eyes connected, they belonged to each other. In
the world where they lived, with its cruel reality, life only
gives small bursts of joy and they didn't want to lose
this one.

From the beginning, they had an uncanny ability
to read each other's mind. When Tula gathered her
few belongings and moved in with him, there was no
ceremony or great proclamation of undying love, because
Wilfred and Tula accepted there could be a day when Old
Massa Nibbs would tear them apart.

They endured the grueling, unending work under the
blazing sun, the fear of the whip, the gripping hunger in
their stomach, and the screams of a parent whose child
was pulled from her arms. On a simple straw bed that sat
on the ground, Wilfred finally had someone to share
his dream.

One day, Wilfred came home with a large chipped jar
and told his wife, "Dis is what we go put the money we
make in. One day we go have enough to buy we freedom."
Each morning they rose and tended their plot, and with
Wilfred's love that land fed them, also yielding produce
they sold at the market. Old Meg had long since died,
but he remembered her words. Coin by coin, the couple
patiently watched their jar fill up. When they looked at
it in the candlelight, it glittered like the chandelier in the
big plantation house.

Tula was thirty-nine when she threw up her breakfast and thought nothing of it. After a week of vomiting, she knew she was with child. For twenty years Wilfred and Tula had slept together, and each month her cycle never ceased. After ten years, they gave up hope of having children, yet Tula never mourned this loss. Before she came to Nibbs plantation, she was a breeder, giving birth to five children from men whose faces she couldn't recall, and breastfed children she didn't want.

Now, as she held onto her stomach, there was a feeling of joy she'd never known. At night, Wilfred lovingly put his hand on his wife's expanding stomach; then with her hand on top of his, they'd rub her protruding belly. They lay like this, in contented silence, night after night, until Tula was seven months' pregnant.

With her hands intertwined with her husband's, Tula finally spoke. "Me want to hold our chile as a free woman. We save all these years—maybe we now have enough money in that jar and this chile will be born free."

Twenty years of coins glittered in a large, chipped jar. Each year they sat on the hard floor in their hut and patiently counted every cent. Each year brought them closer to their dream. Now they needed to know if they could walk away with their free papers and raise their child. That night, they carefully took down the jar and counted coin after coin. Ten. Twenty. Fifty. One hundred. One hundred and twenty-five. They scream, 'We free. We finally free."

For the first time, Wilfred and Tula felt light and joyous. Finally they could imagine a future. They wanted to live close to the sea, wanted to watch their child's imprints on the sand. As the reality of their impending freedom hit them, the two of them felt relief that they'd never see an animal tattoo on their child's back. The night left and the rooster announced a new day, and a very tired Wilfred walked to the big plantation house. If he had a mirror, he'd see the passage of time on the deeply etched lines on his face and the gray hair that dotted his head.

From her lofty position on the balcony of the big plantation house, Betsy spent most mornings languidly observing the comings and goings of the plantation in one of her beautiful gowns. Had her skin not been as dark as the night, one would have thought from her behaviour that she was Massa's wife, but she held a more important role—Betsy was Massa's most beloved mistress —Betsy was Young Nibbs's obsession.

Wilfred and Betsy were born three days apart on the Nibbs plantation. They crawled on the same day; their first words were the same; they took their first steps together. From the time she was born, with her large, luminescent eyes and pouty lips, everyone on the plantation knew she was bound for Old Nibbs's bed.

At five years old, Wilfred truly believed he was in love with Betsy and asked her to marry him when she grew up. She smiled coyly, nodding happily as a gleeful Wilfred skipped around her singing, "Me go marry Betsy, me go marry Betsy."

Old Nibbs was in the slave quarters, talking with the overseer when he overheard Wilfred's childish chant. The overseer panicked when Old Nibbs shouted, "Stop," to the two children. Knowing that Old Nibbs owned them, they abruptly stood still, fearfully waiting.

Old Nibbs ignored Wilfred and went to Betsy. He stooped so that they were the same height and took in the contours of her face and the smoothness of her skin. A smile came to his face and he told her to go. As he watched her run away, he instructed the overseer, "That girl will be mine when she becomes a woman. I don't want her working in the fields, and no one is to beat her, 'cause I don't like scars on a woman's skin." That was why Betsy was the only slave on the Nibbs plantation who never knew a day of hard labour.

After Betsy turned thirteen, Old Nibbs returned to the slave barracks each week to watch the curves emerge on her adolescent body. When he saw her breasts blossom, he couldn't wait any longer. No one else was going to claim his prize. It was daylight when the overseer grabbed Betsy and took her, kicking and biting, to Old Nibbs.

Finally, alone with his fantasy, the old man, tore her old, tattered dress from her. "I'm going to have to dress you in fine garments," he said. And kept his promise.

Island people were accustomed to the stories like Betsy's but were shocked when the old man didn't tire of her after a few months. Old Nibbs was known for his love of dark women, but he flabbergasted everyone —moving her into the big house—treating her like his wife.

After he passed away, his only son inherited the estate. But Old Nibbs left a special clause in his will, ensuring Betsy's care. He bequeathed her the large, luxurious room she occupied in the big plantation house and a stipend to ensure that she lived in style, never having to work in the fields.

Within six months of his father's death, a very frustrated Young Nibbs, who couldn't understand how to run a plantation, visited Betsy's room, curious to understand why his father added a clause in his will to care for a slave woman. Once the son touched her, like his father, he claimed her for himself. Shortly after that visit, everyone on the plantation was shocked when he fired the overseer. The plantation ran more smoothly, and there were whispers that Betsy had influence over Young Nibbs.

Betsy's life was different than that of all the other slaves. She'd long adopted the clipped speech of the English, sleeping on a comfortable bed adorned with silky sheets—a far cry from the old straw-filled sack where she once slept. Her smooth skin held the lustre of a black pearl, and she had no tattoo unlike the other slaves. The envy of every slave, Betsy had become a legend throughout the island.

Over ten years ago, when Tula was lent to another plantation to work, Wilfred awoke to insistent loud thumps. He opened the door and was surprised to see someone camouflaged by a large scarf.

"Can I come in?" the woman asked.

A shocked Wilfred immediately recognized Betsy's voice. His eyes grew wide with pleasure when she removed the wrap to reveal a dress that highlighted her perky breasts, and as he drew in his breath, he inhaled her perfume and was immediately intoxicated.

As she looked around the sparse hut, Wilfred started to apologize.

Betsy interrupted him. "Wilfred, don't tell me you've forgotten that I slept on a bed like yours until Old Nibbs dragged me away. I may live in that big house, but I have never forgotten that I am a slave."

Without asking for permission, Betsy sat on the bed. Wilfred watched in shock as she stretched herself on the mattress, like a temptress, and said in a sultry, seductive voice, "Join me, Wilfred."

"Ms. Betsy, that not right. Me one married man. You all beautiful and smell nice, but me can never touch no other woman than me wife."

Betsy ignored him as she continued, "All I ever dream about is being with a man whose skin is as dark as mine."

Realizing he was tempted, Wilfred moved away from her, trying to keep his distance. Betsy, seeing his response, spoke in a steady voice. "It's been lonely. No one knows what's it's been like. Yet everyone on this island thinks I have a wonderful life because I am the slave woman who lives in her own room in the grand plantation house. The real truth is that Nibbs and his father made me into their whore."

"Ms. Betsy, you too fine to call a whore."

She smiled sadly. "If Nibbs ever believed another man touched me, he'd kill me. I know you love your wife and I promise you won't betray her. Just lie next to me 'cause I just need to finally choose someone. I agreed to marry you when we were five— surely that means something. Can you please allow me this request?"

She had no tattoo on her body and Wilfred had many; she was adorned in silk garments and jewels, while Wilfred wore ripped, old clothing; she'd trained her eyes never to reveal her emotions, while his were dulled; she lived in the big house and he lived in the slaves quarters, but he understood her request—she didn't have to explain. Once they were children who played, and that night they were adults who lay side by side. For once she saw her dark skin blending into another. Her dark eyes stared into his own dark eyes as she touched him; her fingers found his face and traced the contours of his cheeks and nose. She felt the large tattoo on his back and gently traced its outline. She put her hand next to his and looked at the similarity of their skin tone.

Betsy sobbed. Not a loud wail but a small sniffle filled with pain and longing. Wilfred put his arms around her. She sighed and they fell asleep. When he awoke, Betsy was no longer in the room. He never spoke about that night to anyone, not even to Tula. When he needed to ask Young Nibbs how much it would cost to purchase his free paper four years ago, Betsy arranged for him to see Massa.

"Wilfred, it looks like you have the money to buy your free paper," Betsy said.

"Betsy, me so darn happy. You know me love real. There is one thing me know for sure, if me leave this plantation, then she a leave too. That baby she carrying going be born free."

"This is a blessed day."

"I'll be free to do what I want and worship what religion I choose."

"Let me tell you a secret, and don't say this to anyone, but I don't believe in Nibbs's God. He and his people tell us there is a God and that we should worship in their church, but I really wonder if there is a God, why would He allow us to live such wretched lives?"

Wilfred smiled. "Your secret is safe with me."

Betsy escorted him into Young Nibbs's sterile study. When the owner of the plantation saw the dark, gray-haired man carrying a jar filled with coins, he twisted his mouth. Wilfred watched in amazement when Betsy went over to him and put her hand on his shoulder, and he quickly relaxed.

Betsy looked into Wilfred's eyes and nodded—his cue to speak.

"Here, Massa," Wilfred said, hesitantly placing the jar on his desk. "Me have the money to buy me freedom and me wife freedom."

Young Nibbs methodically counted the money. He formed the coins into two neat piles on his desk, one representing the cost of Wilfred and the other Tula.

When he finished, he stared at the two piles. With each second that passed, Wilfred heard his heart beating and he wondered if Young Nibbs also heard its loud thud. Finally, Young Nibbs spoke in his impeccable English accent.

"Wilfred, you and your wife are commendable Negroes. I have counted £125, and although this is a considerable sum, this is only enough to buy your freedom. You are worth £75 and Tula is worth £150. You will need more money to buy Tula."

"What you mean, Massa? Last time we talk, you say it go cost £125 for us two."

"Wilfred, that was before your wife became pregnant. With that child inside of her, Tula is now worth £150. You need another £100 to buy her freedom."

"Me don't understand."

"Yes, this might be too complex for your head. Let me state this simply. That child your wife is carrying is my property, and I will not grant her freedom until it is born. If you have a boy, he will be worth £100. This is what I will do for you. I will grant you your freedom today, and your wife will be free on the day she gives birth, but you will have to purchase your child's freedom."

"That not right."

"What you say, boy?"

"Me say me go work hard to purchase me chile freedom."

Young Nibbs nodded and grabbed some paper from his desk. Wilfred watched as he briskly wrote the words that stated Wilfred was no longer in bondage. This was his life's dream, but he wasn't sure if he felt joy or sadness, because there was no paper for Tula.

Wilfred's hand, dark and aromatic as a newly ploughed field, contrasted with the smooth, white paper. His gentle grasp, like a father tenderly holding his child, ensured there were no creases, smudges or finger marks because he wanted to keep this paper in pristine condition. This sheet, Wilfred's lifelong dream, would eventually disintegrate into a fine dust—the words forgotten—but on that day, the ink's dark and distinct markings contrasted with the paper that carried substantive words proclaiming Wilfred was now a free man.

Tula was sitting on the chair, waiting impatiently. She expected to see uncontained joy; instead, there was a man cradling a piece of paper. A heavy silence filled the room. One paper meant one person was free.

"Who he give the freedom to?" she finally asked.

"Me have me free paper, but Young Nibbs say you go have your free paper after the baby born. But we have to buy our chile freedom."

"A what you mean?"

"He say the chile can fetch lots of money and it belong to him."

"That man real bad-minded. How would he like if someone sell him chile?"

"He sell the ones he make with Betsy. She never held one of them."

"This is we chile. This not fair."

Wilfred touched her stomach. "Me promise that our chile will be free. Me go find a way."

Tula felt a sharp pain and yelled, "The baby a come." With great excitement, Wilfred rushed to his wife's side. The afternoon passed and the night came; then the dark became light, and as the sun rose, the day got hotter and sweat trickled down the side of Wilfred's face, but no child cried and his wife's voice wasn't strong. A worried Wilfred waited, neither bothering to eat or drink, hoping that he'd hear his child's cry. The sun moved past its highest peak when the midwife finally told the agitated father-to-be that the baby didn't want to come out of the womb. Wilfred believed that if the child wasn't born into slavery, it'd ease more freely down Tula's womb. He cursed himself; he cursed Young Nibbs; he cursed life because he didn't have enough money to buy his baby's free paper.

As the hours passed, Tula's body tired. She began to lose strength. Fearing the worst, the worried midwife asked Wilfred to come into the room. When he saw Tula's state, all the blood in his body went cold, but he couldn't let her see his fear. With all the strength of spirit he could muster, a worried Wilfred sat next to Tula and held her feeble hand.

"Remember when we meet?" he asked. "How me look at you and know life go be different. Me can't live without you."

"Wilfred, me 'fraid bad this chile is sucking the life out of me."

"Just push and let it come."

"Wilfred, if me don't make it, promise me that you make sure that we chile get it free paper. Me can't die, knowing we chile go live on this plantation and one day have an animal on its back."

"Tula, don't talk like this."

Tula smiled weakly, and with her remaining strength she pushed the baby out. The midwife yelled, "It's a boy."

With sweat pouring from her body, Tula looked at her husband and said, "Call him Miracle."

"You go be fine."

"This chile is me last gift to you. Just make sure he get he free paper."

"Tula, me love, the baby done born. You go be fine."

"Me can feel me body go weak. Me don't want to leave 'cause our love real."

"Don't keep talking about leaving."

"Wilfred, me have one more thing to ask of you. Promise me that you won't bury me on this plantation. Me now a free woman and me need to be far from this place. Me don't want them to throw me in a pit like all the other dead slaves. They don't even treat us right in death."

There was a hushed silence in the slave quarters when Betsy made her way in a somber black dress to Wilfred's and Tula's cabin. Wilfred was sitting with his son in his arms. Water flowed so freely down his face that the baby was soaked with tears. She gently took the child from

him, dried him and wrapped him in a beautiful
cotton blanket.

Wilfred didn't even look at her. He just stared blankly.
They looked like a strange pair—she in her expensive silk
gown and he dressed in his tattered, old grey shirt. After
an indeterminate silence, she placed a blue pouch on his
lap; the material appeared to glow against his
old clothing.

"It's my gift to you," she said.

Wilfred looked blankly at it. Betsy pulled the cord to
reveal a gold chain with an ornate pendant decorated with
dazzling jewels and gems. Wilfred stared at it in disbelief.

"Betsy, a what is this? You steal this? Put it back before
Massa discover them gone. He go kill you if he find out."

"Wilfred, don't worry. Old Nibbs gave them to me. He
won them when he was gambling."

"You serious?"

"Yes, all the whites on the island know that I legally
own these jewels because Old Nibbs put them on my
neck and told them it was mine."

"Me can't accept this."

"It's a gift, so you can't say no."

"Yes, me can."

"You don't have enough money to buy your son's
freedom and fulfill your wife's dying request, but I do.
I should have given this to you months ago, and maybe
Tula would still be alive."

"Betsy, me can't take your precious stuff. This is enough
for you to buy your own freedom."

"You must know by now that Nibbs will never grant me my freedom. And that is why you must take this gift and buy your son's freedom."

"Betsy, no. Me really can't."

"Wilfred, I am a slave. This trinket means nothing to me. I ask myself all the time, why would a man give me jewelry that I can't wear and not give me freedom that I can cherish?"

"Betsy, things can change."

Betsy's voice was filled with resignation. "In my life in that big house, I've come to understand that this thing called slavery ain't going to end easy—they believe we are made to work in the fields for them. I can help you—let me do that.

"Go to Mr. Walker of the Jolly Plantation. Tell him that I'm willing to sell him his family heirloom for £150 and the land on the hill. When you return, give Nibbs the £100 for Miracle's freedom and use the rest to build your home. I want you to live on that land. Raise your child there, and bury your wife on that hill. Give her the dignity she deserves."

"Betsy, this is too much."

"We can never give enough in life. Wilfred, build a new life far from this plantation. In that place, you will hear a silence so pure that you think there is something called peace. If Nibbs ever gives me freedom, I will join you on that land."

Later that day, Betsy became the owner of a piece of land, and Wilfred left Nibbs's plantation with the free

paper for his son and the body of his beloved wife. Far
from the plantation, he lifted his newborn son high into
the air so that Miracle could see the aqua sea glittering in
the sunlight, and told his only child, "You free, boy." As he
touched his child's smooth skin, he added, "I promise you
will never feel a whip."

Massa Nibbs allowed the slaves off the plantation to
attend Tula's burial. Wilfred laid his wife's body in the
soil, with a stake to mark the spot. Betsy stood next to
Wilfred during the internment. On a wooden tombstone
Wilfred inscribed these words:

On this mount lay Tula

Beloved wife of Wilfred

Mother of Miracle

May your feet roam this mount

Alas, freedom is yours

Not far from his wife's grave Wilfred built a small
cabin and planted crops. A few months later a heart-
broken friend of his, a man still enslaved on Nibbs's
plantation—not wanting his twelve-year-old son to be
thrown into the unmarked burial pit for slaves—asked if
he could bury him next to Tula. As Betsy owned the land,
Wilfred checked with her. She agreed. Another marker

was placed close to Tula's grave. Within a week of that request, a slave from a neighbouring plantation asked if she could bury her husband. Again, Betsy acquiesced. With time, word spread about the burial ground that the people called Mount Tula and Betsy never refused any request. Wooden tombstones engraved with the names of the slaves who died dotted Mount Tula.

It was with great grief when Wilfred buried Betsy on that hill. Malaria took her swiftly and quickly. To be buried there was her last request. A somber Young Nibbs finally allowed her to make a decision. It was the largest funeral the island ever saw, as slaves from across the island came to honour the woman who gave them a burial ground.

Betsy bequeathed Mount Tula to the slaves. Wilfred made sure this legacy continued so his people could find peace in death, far from the plantations. In this place, a sweet breeze told them they could finally rest. Eventually, the story of Tula and Wilfred was forgotten and Mount Tula became known as Montula

Hundreds of spirits found peace in this burial ground, and each person carried a story that was unique and timeless. In this place, Betsy lies. Her children, the ones she never held, also made their way to Montula. Here hundreds more slaves joined their kin.

On August 1, 1834, long after Tula, Betsy and Wilfred passed, a group of people made their way to Montula to tell their Ancestors they were finally free. The spirits of Tula, Betsy, Wilfred, Miracle and all the other slaves buried on this land rose high into the sky, celebrating. In the shadows of that night, the spirits of Wilfred and Betsy danced for hours because slavery was abolished.

After emancipation, Montula was no longer needed. The folks on the island ceased burying their loved ones at this informal graveyard. Eventually, people no longer remembered that their Ancestors lay deep in this ground at this forgotten site. The legacy of Montula was buried. The wooden markers returned to the earth, but the stories of those who rest on this hill are still there, drifting in the wind.

CHAPTER ELEVEN

Coming Home

Hayden finds himself on a plane returning to Antigua. His mind anxiously replaying recent events: the phone call, his father's frightened voice and then a loud thump. The phone lies forlornly on the floor. His father is screaming his name, but he can't pick it up. Finally, with the phone at his ear, he hears his father repeat the words he'd never thought to hear—mother, cancer, inoperable, stage four, three months. Sheer instinct leads him to answer, "I'm coming home right away."

It takes Hayden two weeks to wrap up his life abroad. His workplace suggests he take a leave of absence, but in a crisis like this Hayden doesn't want to be bound by another's rule and time limits. He's thankful his father reassured him that he'll be there for him financially during this period. Each night he dials the familiar phone number of his Antiguan home and speaks with his mother. Her frail voice soothes him. After he hangs up, he stares vacantly at the wall, chastising himself for having stayed away so long. A part of him refuses to accept that he is losing his mother; he wants to believe there is still hope.

Over ten years have passed since Hayden left Antigua with a vague understanding of life. At that time he was a teenager in love with a woman his family disliked. Along that way, he lost that love, found his professional calling and grew up. On foreign soil, he made friends and gained a new perspective about his upbringing, which allowed his relationship with his mother to flourish. He'd learned to keep his female choices to himself so that he didn't have to deal with her meddling. He discovered her innate shyness, her love of classical music, her joy of travel and her deep love for her children.

As the plane glides across the Atlantic, Hayden sees the vast blue of the ocean from the window. Seated next to a stranger who is deeply absorbed in a book, he remembers it's Sunday and fondly reminisces about the sweet slowness of a Caribbean Sunday as it unfolds from the languid morning breakfast of salt fish, accompanied with freshly baked bread, to an afternoon trip to the beach. He recalls the simple joy of capping off the day with a drive to the ice cream parlour for a delightful helping of that sweet, tasty dessert; there he'd always bump into a friend and have a quick chat. Seated on that plane amongst strangers, Hayden has a flashback to his youth when he made tamarind stew with Kai.

It's been two years since Brittany's wedding. He still regrets he didn't call her. As the plane makes its way homeward bound, he can't help but think about Kai.

The aircraft begins its descent in heavy cloud cover. Despite his long absence and his desire to feel the hot Caribbean sun burning his skin, the weather doesn't cooperate. Instead, he's greeted with showers. The moist rain touches him and relieves the heat as he walks along the tarmac. With each footstep, a dormant emotion reawakens as Hayden instinctively begins easing into the pulse of the tropics.

He recognizes some of the people working at the airport, and they warmly greet him. One or two enquire about his mother; it's these small gestures that remind Hayden about the delicious warmth of this small community.

As he stands at the carousel, waiting for his luggage, Hayden remembers that his father used to plead with him to come home—wanting him to work in the family business. Eventually, he realized Hayden wanted to pursue his architectural career. Around that time, Melanie, his father's very capable daughter, a very adept business-woman, became more involved in the business, and his father stopped asking Hayden to come home.

For two years, father and son hadn't seen each other. It was not because there was a feud; it was more complex. They were strangers; their relationship had grown into a strained silence. Hayden never knew that his father was deeply pained about their tense relationship. On Saturday afternoons he laughed amongst his friends, appearing like the proud father, boasting about his son's achievements, never revealing how troubling Hayden's decision to stay away from the island was. This was something he kept deeply buried; too painful to store in a container and too large to put in a box. While his friends' kids frequently visited the island, Hayden only returned for weddings and funerals.

Thomas only heard his son's voice on the phone, wishing him a "Merry Christmas" and "Happy Birthday." His son never called to say, "Hi," and as the years passed, he fervently yearned for a surprise call. He was jealous of Hayden's relationship with his mother—not just in frequent phone calls but also in trips. He was shocked when his wife packed her suitcase to go to Italy with Hayden one year, and then the following year the two of them went to Spain.

Once both children no longer lived at home, Thomas tired of the pretense of his marriage and told his wife he was moving out. Catherine cried for hours, worried about what people would say, but he promised her he'd attend all social gatherings with her. She nodded because this arrangement allowed her to hold her head up high in church.

Although Hayden's father stopped caring about
who said what, he knew there was a delicate balance of
propriety he must walk. He built himself a luxurious
home, with a fabulous view of the Caribbean Sea, where
he entertained his friends and latest mistress. However,
whenever Catherine needed him—for a wedding, funeral
or church event—he dutifully donned his suit and held
her hand as her escort. The truth was, Thomas knew very
little about his wife's life—not having been around to
notice her lack of appetite or rapid weight loss.

In a frazzled state their daughter, Melanie, came to
him one day. Knowing her usual composure, he instinctively anticipated something was seriously wrong. In his
impersonal office, where he negotiated his business deals,
he learned of his wife's critical illness. Melanie's words
stunned him, and he stared at the floor for a long time in
disbelief. He wasn't aware of anything other than that his
level-headed daughter guided him to a seat. After their
years of separation, he didn't know how to approach his
wife. He did the only thing he could; he picked up the
phone and called his son. Hayden screamed, "No!" And
it pained Thomas immensely that he couldn't tell him his
mother was going to be all right.

As soon as his son clears customs, Thomas greets him.
The two men silently assess each other. The last time they
were together was at Brittany's wedding. Hayden's father's
eyes mist when he sees his child, the one who looks so
much like him. His green eyes meet the ones his son

inherited, and Thomas hears his father's voice warning him he needed to stop his selfishness and think about his family. As he stands at the airport, amongst strangers, every broken promise Thomas made comes back to him. He and his son walk to the car in silence.

"How is she doing?" Hayden finally asks when they're sitting in the car.

"She's excited to see you," his father replies.

"I can't believe it's this bad . . ." Hayden begins, but his father interrupts, "Say no more. All that matters is that you're here."

Hayden is perturbed. "I should have come home more often."

"Stop thinking this way. You did what you needed to do." His father pauses before continuing, "She is very excited to see you. She is constantly telling the nurses that her tall, handsome son is coming home and warns them not to fall in love with you."

The conversation ends—their usual silence envelops the car. In his zeal to be at his mother's bedside, Hayden doesn't notice the changes that have occurred on the island. The simplicity of the life he once knew was still there, but the landscape was transforming.

There are bigger homes, taller buildings, shopping malls and traffic congestion. If Hayden had looked out the window, his eyes would have glistened with joy— reminded of the inordinate beauty of this Caribbean gem, with its sweeping hills and bright foliage. But he is so caught up in his pain that he doesn't notice anything, and it doesn't register that the island is alive with the brilliant red of his mother's favourite flower.

Catherine is sitting in the bed, reading her Bible, when she hears the creak from the front door opening. She knows the sound of the loud footsteps belong to Hayden. Her feeble voice momentarily emboldened, she calls, "Hayden, is that you? Is my son finally home?" Her words are like a lasso, pulling him to her. He is overcome with emotion when he sees her emaciated body, but not wanting her to see his emotional state he holds back his desire to cry. Although her thinness overwhelms him, he is stunned that the illness has not ravaged her face, and in some strange twist of fate, her beauty is preserved—in stark contrast to the rest of her diseased body. Without hesitation, he wraps his arms around her thin shoulders with the same tenderness she had for him when he was a child.

From the doorway, Thomas sees his wife glowing with Hayden at her side and leaves the room. Hayden stays until she falls asleep. Once she does, he makes his way to his old bedroom. The dull echo of his footsteps on the well-polished floor resounds through the empty house. Hayden stops and observes, with pleasure, the grand-estate home that is his family's pride. His professional eye notes the high ceiling, the intricate stonework and the large airy windows. Despite the classic perfection of the design and the tasty decor, the house feels like a relic. He remembers how empty it felt for years, long before he left the island. It saddens him that his mother's illness put a further pall on this beautiful building.

Patiently waiting for his return, Hayden's bedroom looks just as it always did. His suitcase is in the corner and he unpacks his things, desperately trying to stave off his thoughts, fearful of finally acknowledging the extent of his mother's illness. With nothing but a sense of despair, Hayden desperately wants to escape. One foot follows the other until he is standing on the veranda, looking at the view that captivated him as a child. It is early evening, and despite his pain, he is awestruck by the moon's iridescent beams dancing playfully on the water.

"Have you forgotten how spectacular it is?"

Hayden turns. His father is sitting alone on the balcony. Thomas immediately sees his son's distraught state and puts his hand on his shoulder. Surprised at the strength of his hand, Hayden is immediately comforted.

His father gently asks, "Are you okay, son?"

"This isn't easy. I can't believe she is in such a bad state."

"She's going down rapidly. We didn't expect that. But she is very happy you've come home to be with her. She really needs you now."

"I'm here for her."

"Let's just make your mother as happy as possible."

"We will." And they slip into silence.

After a few moments his father speaks, "It's so peaceful here."

"Yes, it is. I'd forgotten how relaxing it is."

"It was your favourite spot when you were a child."

His words surprise Hayden, for he couldn't remember his father being around much. He tells him, "I used to snuggle into Mommy's lap and we'd watch the boats sail into the harbour."

There is silence again.

Hayden then looks at his father, "Where's Melanie? I thought she'd be here by now. I'm really looking forward to seeing her."

"She'll be here shortly." Thomas hesitates a moment before he continues. "She's not dealing with your mother's illness very well."

"I never imagined I'd have to see her again under these circumstances."

Father and son sit on the balcony and silently wait.

Twenty minutes later, Hayden anxiously hugs Melanie. Brother and sister look awkwardly at each other, trying to think of something to say. Melanie left home when he was twelve and they've only occasionally seen each other as adults. They feel more like strangers than siblings and are glad when the nurse approaches with news that their mother is awake.

Melanie quickly hugs her mother, then walks over to the window, where she looks out. She doesn't speak to her mother; she doesn't look at her mother; she stands uncomfortably in the corner. Catherine looks at Hayden, and he knows she is silently pleading with him to go to his sister. A few minutes later he takes his sister's hand and leads her to a quiet place in the house.

"Are you okay?" he asks.

Melanie collapses into his arms. "I'm so happy you're here," she sobs. "I can't do this on my own. It's been so hard and I have no one to talk to."

Hayden puts his arm around his big sister. "It'll be okay."

She pleads, "Promise me, you won't go. I really need you now."

"I'm not leaving, Melanie. I'm here and I'm not going anywhere."

"How can you be so strong? Don't you realize our mother is dying?"

Hayden's body goes cold. Then it gets hot. He looks in one direction. Then he turns and looks in the next; he can't run; this is real. He's shocked when he hears himself scream, "It hurts Melanie. It hurts so bad! At least you've been with her and you've been in her life, but I've hardly seen her since I've finished school. I've so much guilt because I haven't been around."

Hayden is no longer calm. Collapsing into his sister's arms, he cries for the first time since learning about his mother's illness. Finally, he is with someone who under-stands. His sister puts her arms around him; he puts his around her. Brother and sister hold tight to each other.

Once they compose themselves, they go outside to the veranda where they see their father waiting. They're unsure if he'd heard their meltdown. He gives no indication if he had. Father, daughter and son sit outside; no one speaks; there is quiet. The maid brings them food and drinks; this distraction eases the strain, and slowly words start to flow. They don't speak about their mother. His father and sister tease Hayden about staying away for so long and becoming a foreigner. There is laughter when they tell him about the latest antics of a friend, and the conversation gets very heated when they speak about the recent political scandals. It's been a long time since the house of his birth has been filled with chatter. Its loneliness begins to ease.

Hayden seldom leaves his mother's side—going to her as soon as he wakes. A smile always comes to her face when she sees him. They pass the time playing cards, reminiscing about their trips. The house stirs with visitors. Hayden is once again greeting his aunts, uncles and cousins; his mother's church friends are often at her bedside, while her bridge cronies still insist on playing cards. They set up a table in her bedroom, where the four of them bid for trump. Once his mother tires, Hayden finds himself sitting at the table, the designated substitute for his mother. The women gush over him as they deal the cards. They all try to see if he's interested in meeting their beautiful daughter or niece.

One day, when the sky is dark with clouds and the soothing sound of the rain on the roof keeps visitors away, Catherine asks Hayden to read to her. He leafs through the books in her room. Coming upon *Unspoken Tales* by Kai Robbins, he gently pulls it from the bookcase and nestles it in his hands. His mother sees him lingering over the title and notices his mood shift. Suspecting what caused it, she feels uncomfortable. Catherine is aware that the clock will stop at any moment and realizes that it's time she makes sure it moves forward for him.

She hesitantly asks, "What book are you looking at?"

"*Unspoken Tales*," he replies, unsure if she knows the name of the author.

"Can you read that to me?" she asks. "There are some really excellent short stories in that book."

He looks at her for a long time, a million unvoiced thoughts speeding through his mind before he calmly asks, "Do you know this book is written by Kai?"

"Yes. The girl has done well for herself despite her upbringing. Have you read it?"

"I've read everything she's written."

There's an uncomfortable silence before she continues. "Kai is talented. Can you read me the story?"

Something inside of him wants to explode, but he keeps his emotions in check, reminding himself it was a long time ago. Catherine notes his discomfort but can't face him. However, she's very aware that as he reads the book, his voice becomes relaxed. She hopes he's forgotten that she hated Kai as much as he loved her.

As the days turn to weeks, Hayden reimmerses himself in his Caribbean heritage with a sense of contentment. He enjoys seeing his mother smile when Melanie's kids visit, and he feels a pang of remorse that he doesn't have any children as he watches them clamour onto the bed to talk with their grandmother.

In their sorrow he and his sister find each other. Not a demonstrative person, Melanie continues to have a very hard time dealing with their mother's sickness, but he helps her navigate this period. After his meltdown, he becomes her anchor. Although she visits her mother daily, they are brief and abrupt visits that always leave her teary eyed.

Brother and sister are pulled to the balcony, finding solace in the spectacular view—something they seldom did together because of their age gap and the fact that they didn't really know each other. They talk about their upbringing. In their raw emotional state they finally speak about the pain of their parent's strange relationship. The words that leave their lips are the same; their heartaches are similar, and they finally realize this is a bond only they can share.

With time alone, Hayden allows himself to think about Kai. He has an overwhelming desire to call her but remembers her reaction at Brittany's wedding and is unsure. With the island so small, Hayden knows that it's inevitable that one day he'll bump into her, and he desperately hopes for it to be sooner rather than later. Now a man, he acknowledges the emptiness of nights with the wrong person; he misses the intimacy of loving one woman and longingly remembers the strength of their bond.

Although his mother's illness exhausts him, Hayden is restless. At night while she sleeps, he finds himself sitting with his father on the gallery, looking at the spectacular view, as they become reacquainted with each other. Some evenings, they escape to a local bar for much-needed laughter. At other times, they contentedly sit and watch the stars from the balcony, languidly enjoying the sound of the crickets filling the air.

On one of these quiet evenings, Thomas looks at his only son and says in a very serious tone, "It's time we speak."

Hayden is about to respond. But his father continues, "I need to be totally honest with you. You know that I don't live in this house anymore, and I haven't lived here for a long time. But your mother's illness has brought me back to this house, and I've been spending more time on this patio. I think this view makes you do a lot of thinking."

He sees the pensive look on his father's face, and decides to stay silent.

"It's so good to have you here. I know it means the world to your mother, but for my own selfish reasons it also means a lot to me. I finally have the chance to know you. I don't like it that my child is a stranger to me. You're an adult now, and I can openly acknowledge that I was not a good father or husband. In all honesty, my work and friends took precedence over my family.

"I say this with the utmost sincerity. Love left my marriage long ago, but your mother's illness hit me. Looking back, we were two people who should never have been together. I did a lot of bad things to her, but I honestly want her to be comfortable during her last days.

It's the least I can do for her—she gave me two
wonderful children.

"In the end, she brought you home and it's so good to
have you here. It's so nice to look into eyes that are like
my own." His father is quiet before looking earnestly at
Hayden. "Have you thought about staying? You could do
so much with your credentials. You don't have to work
with me. There are other opportunities out there."

Son turns to his father and says, "Coming back made
me realize that this is home."

"I've always said nothing 'tall' sweeter than this island.
It's paradise."

"I agree. It's time for me to be with my family."

"That's good." There is a moment of silence before his
father adds, "Tomorrow, we'll go to my lawyer. I will sign
the deed of this house to you. I think you love this house
more than your mother or me. It truly belongs to you.
This will be your home."

On a Sunday afternoon Hayden's mother looks at her
son. "Hayden, I long to eat some coconut ice cream," she
says. "Can you get me some?"

That is how Hayden finds himself standing in the
line-up at the island's favourite ice cream parlour,
patiently waiting his turn. With his mind preoccupied
solely with getting his mother's ice cream, he doesn't look
to see if he knows anyone in line.

CHAPTER TWELVE

There Is No Ending

I'm at the front of the line at the ice cream parlour, and as soon as I purchase my cone, I turn around and there is Hayden. Despite the years of silence between us, he looks the same to me. And once again, I feel like a fifteen-year-old girl, standing in his family store—a young woman at a loss for words. A large smile comes to his face when he sees me. We stare at each other for several minutes. Then someone behind him yells, "Excuse me. Are you getting ice cream or talking?"

We both laugh sheepishly as Hayden steps out of the line.

"Hi, Kai," he finally says. "You haven't aged. You're still as sweet as tamarind stew."

"Thanks." I blush. "You haven't changed either."

"That's what everyone says. But I know I have."

"I'm sorry to hear about your mother," I add, safely changing the subject.

"Thanks," he replies.

"How is she doing?"

"She has good days and bad. It's not easy." He continues, "No one tells you how hard it is to deal with until you're living with it."

"All that matters is that you're here for her."

"I wouldn't be anywhere else." Then he switches back to the earlier subject. "It's so good to see you. I've thought about calling, but to be honest, the past few weeks have been crazy."

"You don't need to explain. I understand."

"There is so much that I want to say . . ."

"Don't worry, Hayden. There'll be time."

"When I was a young man, a sage girl told me to follow my passion and not my father's wishes. I listened to her. So I'm listening to her again because she was right then."

We smile so easily at each other.

"Kai, I've heard that you've moved."

"Yes, I live in this beautiful, airy house at Montula. I know this may sound crazy, but it has many of the ideas you suggested I incorporate into my future home, eons ago. I finally have my own writing room. And in the yard

I've built a statue as a tribute to our Ancestors, like you said I should. It surprised me that it became an attraction. People from all over the island come to look at it."

"I'm glad to know I had a good influence on your life. I've heard about it and plan to visit one day."

"That'd be great."

"Will you take me on a tour of your new home when I come?"

He looks earnestly at me, with his beautiful eyes as enticing as the Caribbean Sea.

"Yes," I reply. "I'll be happy to show you around."

I don't know how I leave his side, but I do. I drive straight home. The Ancestors are singing. They whisper something so special in my ear. I get up and go to the kitchen. I place the tamarinds in a pot and let them simmer. Then I go outside to my veranda and wait.

Hayden's mother hears his footsteps. She immediately notes his lighter mood but doesn't speak. Her son smiles sweetly as he gently lifts her frail body to the balcony, where there is a container of ice cream and two cups. She hasn't been outside for a few weeks because she's doesn't have any strength, but she's glad to get away from her room.

He scoops out a serving for him and one for her. A cool breeze blows as they eat their favourite dessert. In front of them the beguiling Caribbean Sea glistens at sunset. His mother inhales the fresh breeze, her eyes watering as she breathes a sigh of deep satisfaction, noting that the island is alight with the brilliant red flowers of the flamboyant tree.

She touches Hayden's sleeve, points to the tree and speaks in an ethereal voice. "Hayden, promise me I'll have some flamboyant flowers at my funeral. I know it's unorthodox, but that's what I want. You know, I had many dreams. Only two came true, you and your sister—that's why I'm asking you to make sure I have them at my funeral."

"Mom, stop being so morbid."

"Hayden, let me speak. I know I will not see another season when the flamboyant tree will bloom. Perhaps that's why I'm so happy, sitting outside with you and watching the yard alive with its flower. Promise me, you'll have some of those flowers on the altar of the church at my funeral?"

Hayden nods. "Nor do I know," she continues, "if I'll ever eat another one of Antigua's sweet mangoes, because they're not in season. I'm savouring everything while I'm still alive. I don't have much time left. I can feel life leaving my body. I never knew what was God's plan. Why does He want to take me so quickly before I even have a chance to hold your child?"

"I don't want to talk about this," he replies.

"I know you don't. But I need to talk. You are the closest person to me. I can't speak to any women from the church or the bridge club. Your sister is so upset she can barely say a word when she sees me. She is just like her father, unable to express her emotions. God knows, your

father and I were never able to speak to each other. You
are my child and the only one who understands me. It is
your dying mother's wish to talk with you."

"Daddy is trying."

"It's late, my son; much too late. It guilt have him now,
but he has been here for me during this time, and by
the grace of God, that means something. I came to this
house when I married him. How I loved him back then!
It's amazing that love can become so twisted; we can't
even stand to be in the same room. I know he never really
loved me, but I don't think he has ever really loved any
woman. He's much too selfish. When you're dying, you
think about your life. I ask myself why God put me here,
because the only good thing I did was make two
beautiful children."

"Don't say that."

"It's true. I had a long, miserable life with your father,
and now I have this drawn-out, painful death. I must have
done something wrong to deserve this." Then her voice
changes and her eyes pierce his. "You saw her didn't you?"

"Who are you talking about?"

"Kai. Did you see her?"

He nods in puzzlement. "How did you know?"

"A mother can see things. The last time I saw you have
that spark in your eyes, you were with her."

Hayden doesn't respond—he doesn't know what to
say. His mother continues, "Hayden, I know you thought
I was a snob. I was taught that her dark skin and where
she lived were beneath me. It's not easy for me to let go

of the things I was taught. But I've come to terms with the fact that the two of you have a real love. I've interfered and made things difficult. Life has taught me that I can't choose your girlfriend or wife. Maybe that's why God is cursing me now."

"Don't say that. That's not true. I was the one who screwed up my relationship with Kai."

"Son, I helped you. I never welcomed her into our home. It was wrong. As I writhe in pain, these are the questions going through my mind."

"That was over ten years ago. Kai and I were children back then."

"You were. And I thought she was your rebellion against me. I'm dying and I won't live to see what you finally decide about her. I do know that you will go to her. After that, I don't know what will happen. If she still makes you smile, then she is the one for you. I know this may sound strange coming from me, but if she is your happiness, claim it. Don't waste your life on the wrong person the way I did with your father. Life is too short. One day you're young, and next thing you know, you're old and you wonder why you didn't seek happiness. I'm getting tired. Take me inside. I need to rest."

Lifting his mother, Hayden marvels at how light she feels. Each day her body has less energy and she grows weaker. It pains him. She falls asleep in his arms and the nurse smiles sympathetically at him as he gently places her on the bed. He returns to the balcony. Darkness has

claimed the island. Without thinking, he jumps into
his car.

I'm waiting for him, like the Ancestors told me.
"I had to see you," he says as he hugs me.
I don't say anything because I'm too afraid to speak.
"If I'm honest with you, will you be honest with me?"
I nod.
"This is so hard, but I have to say it. So many years
have gone by, and I've never stopped thinking about you.
I always wondered how things got so bad that we could
never get back to each other. I've missed what we shared.
Even before I returned, I've thought about contacting you.
It's been lonely out there. I don't know how you feel, but I
would really like it if you'll spend some time with me."
The moon is high in the sky and I see the loneliness
in his eyes. As he stretches his hand out into the divide
between us, I know there is still a deep, abiding love to be
expressed; our spark is infinite, like the skies.
My eyes tell him yes, and we both know there is
nothing more to say. He puts his hand in mine and I lead
him inside. We lie on my bed and look at each other. Our
bodies are not touching, but there is such a comfortable
feeling as we lay together—no words spoken. We move
closer and our lips touch. The kiss deepens. My hands
wander to his back, running down his spine. Everything
feels the same. As I touch him, he touches me. I don't
care—nor do I want to care—about what I'm doing; I

only want to touch Hayden again, and I know in touching
him I'm reawakening us.

We undress each other, slowly undoing the buttons
and removing the clothes from our bodies until there
is nothing left. Then we look at each other's nakedness.
After so many years apart, I see his smooth, golden skin
once more. My hunger for him is different. I watch him
because I want to see him. I look at him. My eyes seek his
unique aqua eyes. My reflection stares back at me. Then
he looks at me and sees his reflection. We stay like that
for a while and then we kiss and kiss and kiss.

When he returns to his family home, the sun is
making its way into the sky and his mother is awake. She
hears his footsteps and calls to him.

"Did you go to her?" she asks.

He hesitates before he replies, "Yes."

"If you still love each other, make it work. I'm leaving
you, son, and all I want is your happiness. Stay with her if
that is what you truly want."

A few days after she spoke those words, Hayden's
mother dies. Her illness does the one thing her life
could not; it brings her family together, as her children
and husband find each other in their deep sorrow. They
rediscover the memories and heartaches distinct to their
bloodline. As much as she fears leaving them, she dies
peacefully—knowing that her family is finally together.
Her husband, son and daughter all saw a side of her that

none knew during her life. Each one of them shed tears when she closed her eyes forever.

I know the exact moment when Hayden's mother dies, even though I'm not with her. The Ancestors tell me she will be joining them shortly. Then the phone rings and I know it's Hayden. Through his sobs, he asks me to come to him and I do.

Before I go to him, I bend my head into the wind; her story merges with the Ancestors; I let their voices sail through me as I thank her for sending Hayden to me.

I sit at Hayden's side at the funeral. Brittany returns for the funeral and is also seated in the pew with us. People stare at me in surprise, because they don't expect me next to Hayden after all these years. It's a beautiful service, with the bold red flowers from the flamboyant tree decorating the altar. People who knew his mother fill the cathedral. They cry as they sing the hymns she requested. Hayden gives the eulogy, accompanied by many sobs as he remembers his mother's sweet and enduring love. Her son, daughter and husband shed genuine tears as the casket sinks into the ground. But they are not the only ones. When a woman dies before all her hair is gray, she is known by many, and they often speculate about what else she might have done if her life were longer.

I know my story with Hayden began before that bright moonlit night on the balcony of Brittany's house. I even believe it started before I looked deeply into his eyes at

his family store. Life has taught me our love was always
there, patiently waiting for us to touch it.

We sway in the breeze as we lie in the hammock
on the balcony of his house where generations of his
kinfolk once lived. Hayden tells me to look. A shooting
star bursts across the sky. He asks me to make a wish.
Then he requests that I share my thought. I say we
must always love each other. With the sweet Antiguan
breeze caressing our skin and the sticky tamarind stew
simmering on the stove, Hayden proposes. I accept.

Hayden is next to me, our bodies carrying the same
heat. Earlier that day, surrounded by those we love, we
hosted a quiet ceremony to celebrate our union. My
mother and Vee cried with joy as I walked down the
aisle in a beautiful white dress. Hayden's father and sister
nodded their approval when he smiled into my eyes. And
Brittany leapt with joy when we kissed to seal
our commitment.

This morning I decided I did not need to speak with
the Ancestors, for I wanted only my voice in my head
when I made my vow of love. I now understand that the
unique essence that is Hayden and me will always fight to
hold onto us. I knew the Ancestors were above, watching
and smiling, as we said, "I do," and I heard them sing
"Alleluia" when we kissed.

I feel the heat of his body as it presses into mine. I
trace the strength of his limbs as he lies next to me. I am

exhausted, yet exhilarated, from our lovemaking. I know I can never have enough of him and of this wondrous emotion. Each time we touch, it feels new, and the excitement always leaves me breathless with anticipation. I leave him in the room and step outside.

With my marriage I have two homes, and I love that my life is filled with endless possibilities. This night, we are at the house at Montula, where I've found peace and creativity surrounded by the sounds of the Ancestors. I stretch my hands out to embrace their spirits; their voices rise to greet me. In the moonlight, the statue appears to be a glistening beacon, with the faces that tell me today will one day merge with yesterday.

The Ancestors' voices are getting stronger, for I hear their words everywhere. It's there in the faces of the people I see. It's as if we can finally embrace them; our past is our present. Their words are alive in our music. It's there in every action of the people.

I see Hayden lying on the bed and I hear the sound of his body as he breathes. The sweet Antiguan breeze is softly caressing my skin as I stand outside. I know I will shortly go to Hayden and lie naked with him. I raise my hands high into the heavens and at the beacon that salutes the Ancestors.

I feel their strength pulsating around me. They always told me that stories have no endings—they go on and on. Each generation will find something new to say. As I stand outside, looking into the immense heavens, I realize I will never be able to count every star, because our universe is continually changing. In humility, I acknowledge that I do not know how my own story will end. I never dreamt I'd return to Hayden and love him with more joy and intensity. My life continues to surprise and thrill me. I've learned that love is truly with no beginning or end—infinite in possibility. The only truth I now understand is that words will go on and on. There is no ending.

Acknowledgements

This book was birthed from my first published short story, "Tamarind Stew." With the help of a writing group, that story and its characters began to take shape. A shout-out to Cheryl, who gave me great advice—move a passage to the prologue.

My father loves to drive around Antigua. Whenever I visit, we put more mileage on his rusted white SUV. One day as he drove along another bumpy road to a place called Montula, he told me this was a forgotten graveyard where slaves were buried. I'd been working on this book and couldn't figure out how to incorporate the Ancestors' voices. As his words filled the air, the entire story came together—as if the Ancestors were literally whispering to me their story. For me, this book truly came to life on that drive.

I can't thank my sister, Nicola, enough for her support and feedback: she read the first draft, and without her critical remarks the book would not be what it is today. Althea Prince has been a great mentor, who pushed me to seek writing excellence. I'm truly thankful to have her in my life. Jackie, thanks for printing drafts when my funds were low and listening to me ramble on our long walks. Barbara, you were there from the beginning—reading and rereading draft after draft. You helped me keep the focus—truly appreciated. Mackenzie, thanks for your keen review and observations.

My rock has been my immediate family, which extends from my parents, brother and sister to my Mississauga family. As always, a thank-you to each and every one of you for the day-to-day support. Uncle Eugene, your optimism further pushed me to keep writing.

A book is a journey, and there are so many people who held your hand in one way or another. Thank you to Louis, Rosie, Dionne, Natalie, Sadie, Tracey, Sandra and Gus. I've been blessed with great friends who have been there for me—I can't say thank-you enough to the women who keep me focused and *listen* to my heart. And if I've missed calling out your name, please know you're still an important piece of my life.

I was further blessed with Margaret Harrell's keen editing eye. Her knowledge of words and language was an immense help to completing the book. Furthermore, her guidance on all things publishing was invaluable.

Finally, to the Universe, thank you for allowing me to nurture my creative voice.

Peace to all, Gayle

About the Author

Gayle Gonsalves is an established storyteller. Her short stories have appeared in numerous anthologies, such as The Bluelight Corner, In the Black, The Black Notes, Tongues of the Ocean and So the Nailhead Bend, So the Story Ends. Her first book, Painting Pictures and Other Stories, is a collection of lyrical stories of love and betrayal, reflection and reconciliation in Canada and Antigua. My Stories Have No Endings is her first novel. Gonsalves enriches her narrative by evoking colours, textures and shapes with words. She has lived in Antigua and Canada. Gonsalves is a graduate of York University in Toronto, where she currently lives and writes.

Made in the USA
Monee, IL
19 March 2021